THE CASE

Edward Minyard

Stay Prepared!

DEDICATION

This book is dedicated to my darling wife, Joy Tarbell—my greatest fan and supporter. And to my best friend, Roger Dorethy, for encouraging me to write

Acknowledgements

I would like to thank my wife, Joy Tarbell, for her patience and support. Without her, I would not have the peace of mind – or the quiet space – to write this book.

Special thanks to my best friend, Roger Lee Dorethy. He has been my sounding board, throughout the development of my concept and characters, my inspiration when I had none, and the 'quality assurance' editor, as I wrote each scene or chapter.

Thank you to my friend Ronnie Martin, a retired Major of the St. Bernard Parish, LA Sheriff's Office, and SWAT consultant for the television series, 'CSI New Orleans.' Ronnie has been my technical backstop on the cop stuff.

A hearty thanks to Kevin McMenimen, former FBI, for his input – and for allowing me to use him as a character!

Special thanks to my Bro-in-Law, Dr. Larry 'Slowhand' Katz, for his editorial input, saving me from looking like an uneducated dolt.

Lastly, to the families of Gary Harker and Cody James – may you someday find answers.

Prologue

Undercover—it can be a nasty business. Constantly meeting new people is always interesting. Realizing that you may need to send them to prison—or kill them—adds a whole different flavor.

Rob Anderson knows his job. And he loves his work. It's all he has, really. No family to speak of. No 'significant other'—though many 'insignificant others' tend to come and go. Rob likes it like that. No baggage. Great memories. Not-so-great memories. All part of the tapestry that makes up the life of Rob Anderson. A former US Army Ranger and Special Agent with the Drug Enforcement Administration, Rob lives for the thrill of the work—the intrigue, the suspense—and the adrenaline associated with knowing one wrong word or move could cost him everything—including his life.

And so it almost did, in Post-Katrina New Orleans, because of his dogged determination to close a twenty-five year old cold case.

CHAPTER 1—Calm Under Fire

'CALM UNDER FIRE'—These are words used by Rob Anderson's Unit Commander in Vietnam, in Rob's Bronze Star Citation. Rob had been a Ranger, in that conflict, assigned to recon duties. As such, he had plenty of opportunities to develop that trait. And practice it. And perfect it. It served him well then and has served him well since—the weirder things got; the calmer Rob became. Some viewed that as a trait of a bad-ass operator. Rob felt it was more like a genetic misfire. Still, he was alive because of it—and had remained so, through plenty of opportunities for the opposite outcome.

Upon his return to 'The World' in 1970, after two tours, Rob re-upped—on condition of changing his Military Occupational Specialty to 31-Bravo—Military Police. Rob had already earned his associate degree in Criminal Justice prior to enlisting in the US Army in 1968, so it wasn't such a strange career move, even for a Jungle Warrior. After two more years and another stripe on his sleeve, Sergeant Rob Anderson applied for and was accepted to the Army's elite Criminal Investigations Division (CID), where he intended to serve out his 20 years, then retire to some backwoods, to become a small-town cop on a no-stress police force.

As the old saying goes: if you want to hear God laugh, make a plan…

As a CID Agent, Rob was assigned to work on one of the biggest problems being faced in the Vietnam Era Army—drug enforcement. Between the guys shipping pot, opium and heroin back from Nam, and the growing Counterculture and easy availability of all those drugs, plus cocaine, LSD, speed and downers here in the States, the Army had serious issues. Rob's job was to get to the root-cause—find the dealers and take them down. This required him to go undercover. To seek out, infiltrate and destroy the operations—much like in Vietnam!

Rob grew his hair out, stopped trimming his mustache, traded his OD Greens for blue jeans—except the field jacket, of course—that was a standard part of the "hippie uniform"—and perfect for concealing his Bianchi shoulder rig, holding his World War II-vintage Remington-Rand M1911 pistol on his left side and two extra mags on the right. This classic had become his preferred weapon for many reasons—reliability, cool factor… and not 'company issue.' His first duty station was outside of Fort Carson, CO. There, he worked with civilian investigators to take down a significant ring of dealers and suppliers. That was his first assignment—but not his only one.

This routine recurred outside of no fewer than six other bases over the next few years.

That set the hook.

During a rather large investigation and take down, outside of and including Fort Ord, CA, Rob was assigned to be part of a Joint Task Force, including State and Federal Agencies. This resulted in a bust of several soldiers and several civilians, who were smuggling large quantities of marijuana, cocaine and speed from Central America and the Panama Canal Zone, directly through 3d Brigade mail room, at Fort Ord. A very big deal, indeed. It also resulted in a new job offer for Rob Anderson—from the United States Drug Enforcement Administration, as a member of one of its elite Mobile Enforcement Teams—part of the DEA's Central Tactical Units (CENTAC) program.

In mid-1979, Rob was included in briefings about a major cocaine smuggling operation, apparently centered in and around the San Francisco Bay Area. DEA had recently concluded an operation in New Orleans, dubbed 'Operation Alligator.' The operation had busted a Nicaraguan trafficker, who advised the Special Agents that he had given another Nicaraguan, called Norwin Menolos, money for cocaine and that he had helped

Menolos smuggle the coke into the New Orleans area, via loads of lumber from Ecuador. Menolos and his family had lavish homes and other property, all around the San Francisco Bay Area. This seemed to confirm that the military transport method of shipment had been only one of many, and that this was a very widespread, elaborate smuggling organization. As it turned out, Rob and the DEA Team had no idea just how elaborate.

At least not ALL the DEA members were aware…

Coming up to the end of his third four-year enlistment contract—Rob made the decision to make the jump, on condition that his twelve years of government service be recognized toward his ultimate retirement goals. And even though he looked like a 25-year-old freak, he was actually 32 years old. How much longer could he play this young man's game? Time to expand the horizons!

The next few years with the DEA were quite 'eventful.' As Patton once defined war: 'Long periods of boredom, punctuated by moments of sheer terror.' Those 'moments' included several no-bullshit raids, including a few shootouts, resulting in the loss of some very good Agents—and a larger number of very bad criminals. Still, Rob could see that it was a losing battle—the drugs were here to stay. They were a part of every social stratum. Very big, very rich, very well-placed people were involved, apparently including politicians and law enforcement officers. For Rob Anderson, the writing was on the wall—time to stop pissing into the wind. Then came 'the case.'

CHAPTER 2—The Case

As a part of the Fort Ord bust, investigators uncovered that the trail of drugs led to yet another base—an unlikely one, at that—Rock Island Arsenal, in Illinois. A small base, used primarily for research and weapons development activities. Drugs were moving from California to Illinois via a well-established set of channels, providing a major portion of the supply to most of the central Midwest. In late 1979, Rob transferred to the Operation Clean Sweep Task Force in Rock Island, Illinois. Rock Island is one of four communities that made up the area known as The Quad Cities—called that because of the four cities of Rock Island, IL, Davenport, IA, Moline, IL and Bettendorf, IA, on opposite sides of the Mississippi River. The DEA knew of the operation there, thanks to a cooperative 'potential defendant' in California, who preferred a discrete chat with the DEA and his own warm bed to a used mattress in a Federal Penitentiary. The details were slim—and more than a small bit sketchy—but were considered solid. Enough to act on, certainly. Enough to have Rob Anderson quietly deployed halfway across the country, driving his new, California-registered '79 Camaro. His cover was as a large-scale dealer—he had to look the part!

Like everywhere else in the country, drugs were rampant in the Midwest—and quite lucrative for the smugglers and dealers. According to the snitch in California, two of those dealers had become very well established throughout the region—main suppliers of just about anything the connoisseur of fine drugs could desire.

Gary Harker and Cody James had been pals since high school. They were always the cool 'Bad Boys,' living just across the line of the law. Cody always felt that he was just living up to his family traditions—he was the grandson of Frank James, after all. If outlawing was good enough for Frank and Jesse James, who was he to argue? Gary, well, he was just in it for the thrill… and the money, of course. It was through a Nam Vet friend that they were introduced to an Army Officer at Rock Island Arsenal. That Officer had been previously stationed at Fort Ord, California.

Gary and Cody were already involved in the drug community of the Quad Cities, albeit only on a small scale. When they could score in some quantity, they sold to their friends. Otherwise, they scrounged for whatever they could get buzzed on. Meeting this new connection changed everything for them. Seemingly limitless supplies of the finest stuff—they became very popular, and their boundaries expanded. From Chicago to Omaha to St. Louis, they were 'The Go-To Guys.' Until they weren't.

Arriving in Illinois in October 1979, Rob connected with a relatively trustworthy 'CI'—Confidential Informer—named Joey Hill. 'Relatively' being the operative word. Joey had been busted several years earlier on a significant drug rap. Facing up to 25 years in prison, Joey was quick to flip. He threw more people under the bus than a shop supervisor at the Trailways maintenance garage. Joey was also known to spend state and federal drug-buy money to have some grand parties, which didn't result in busts… he just liked to party! Joey was a likeable guy, with a constant smile, a head of slightly receding blonde hair—and a Rolodex filled with hot babes and dope connections. Joey was in the circle of friends with Gary Harker and Cody James—his job was to help get Rob into that circle, too. Rob met Joey at the LeClaire Hotel in Moline, IL.

Chapter 3—Ground Rules

"You must be Joey Hill," Rob said. "no one else could fit the description!"

"And they'd damn well better never try! Must be Roger, right?" answered Joey, "Pleasure to make your acquaintance."

For this mission, Rob had assumed the "nom de guerre" of Roger Lee, a well-placed dealer from the San Francisco Bay Area. Roger had been identified during the Fort Ord bust. He was a recipient of some of the cocaine coming in through the base, but was also suspected of having other, even bigger connections. He had been corralled, then conveniently "disappeared" into the Federal Witness Protection Program. One day out there and doing serious deals, the next—just gone. A perfect cover for the game Rob had in play.

Sitting across from Joey, at a table away from the bar, Rob / Roger took stock of the CI. He noticed the twinkle in his eyes, his affable charm and his comfortable demeanor. He also noticed the leather choker around Joey's neck, with the single row of colored beads hanging from it—white, yellow, green, blue, brown and black.

"Love the necklace," Rob said, sipping his Macallan, "Tang Soo Do?"

Joey's smile widened. "Moo Duk Kwan. Very observant! You study?"

"Dabbled a bit, in Nam," came the lie, "never got too deep." In fact, Rob was a fifth-degree black belt in Chung Moo Kwan Taekwondo—a particularly deadly Korean martial art. True, that he began in Nam, under the tutelage of a Republic of Korea Army instructor named Jung Tae Park. Park was one of the ROK Chief Instructors, assigned to train US and Vietnamese soldiers. His White Horse Division ROK soldiers were badasses, feared by the Viet Cong. But Rob told a lie, when he said that he 'dabbled.' As a Fifth Dan, he was considered a Master of the art. This is a great way to develop that bond needed between agent and informer, Rob thought. Still, the ground rules needed to be a bit more firmly set.

"Let's get a few things out of the way, Joey, before we get to be asshole buddies. This is my game, and we will play by my rules. I only have a couple. First—don't ever lie to me. I can smell bullshit for miles. Next—don't ask about shit that doesn't fit the program. We know each other through mutual friends from the Army. You know my rep and know people who know my operations in California. That's the story and we stick to it. Are we good?"

"All cool here. I'm only in it for the money—and to stay on the street, if you can dig it. Both are tied to me helping you with this gig. Once you're in, I'm way out, man!"

Rob / Roger leaned in close. "One very important message that needs to be subtly conveyed to the folks we are about to get involved with—my reputation includes not being particularly agreeable when fucked over. I will rip off heads and shit down throats—and lose no sleep over it. It's important that certain folks get that message. Starting with you."

Lifting his glass in a toast, the CI grinned and said, "Let the games begin!"

Chapter 4—Strategy

Every sting needs a solid strategy—otherwise, things get very weird, very quickly. Rob's strategy for this mission was really simple. Two major elements: eliminate the existing supply competition; become the supplier. Well, that's how the target would see it, anyway. We had eliminated one of the main sources of illegal drugs with the Fort Ord bust—or so the DEA thought. Yet, Harker and James were not only still IN the game, but they had seemingly UPPED their game. The plan was to get to the main sources while crushing the regional distribution. And these guys weren't the only sources in the area. Rob planned to make them think they were by removing their competitors. Discretely, of course. This would increase the demand for their products, requiring them to expand their supply chain. Which, if things went the right way, would get Rob/Roger in the mix.

Things didn't go the right way.

Rob rolled out of bed at 0500 on that late-October morning, and began his usual ritual—stretching, light calisthenics, a series of kicks, strikes and blocks, while visualizing an opponent—followed by a cool shower, brushing his teeth and carefully trimming his bodacious Peter Max-like mustache. He was proud of that 'stache—he'd had one version or another since his college days. It was damn cool. Once squared away, he went down to the café for coffee and breakfast. Gotta start the day right—Rob never knew how the rest of it would go. On the way, he stopped by the payphone bank, off the lobby. He dialed the local check-in number—a switchboard operator answered:

"Arsenal Pharmaceuticals answering service, may I take a message?"

Cute, Rob thought. "Please let Mr. Hoover know we expect sales to improve, before month end!"

That was all that needed to be said. Rob would repeat some version of this call, three times a week—more if need be.

As he worked on his second cup, Rob scanned the local Daily Dispatch newspaper, looking for 'Homes for Rent' ads. He needed to have a place for his 'flash stash'—a supply of various controlled substances that he could show off to his potential 'customers.' For establishing credibility, ain't nothin' like the real thing, baby. He found a couple of possibles—he'd get the other Task Force operatives to scope them out. Don't need to be in a neighborhood that would come with its own problems, after all. Then, in the persona of 'Roger,' he settled in to wait for

Joey. They had shit to do. In the background, He heard the sounds of The Eagles, singing, 'There's Gonna Be a Heartache Tonight.'

"Yes," Rob thought, "there just might be…"

As planned, Joey rolled up at close to 0800. The man he called Roger climbed into the tricked-out van, with a degree of admiration—all the coolest toys, including a top-of-the line Panasonic 8-track player and six speakers. The back of the van was wall-to-wall shag carpeting, with a bench seat that converted to a bed…for sleeping, of course.

"What's on the agenda, boss?"

"Today," Roger grinned, "you drive me around and give me the lay of the land—cool clubs, who's who… that sort of stuff. Oh, and the names of The James Gang's top competitors and suppliers." Having boned up on Cody's background, that tag was just too obvious to pass up.

"Roger, Roger!" came the reply, with that wiseass grin that was at once irritating and endearing. "We are on it!"

The rest of the morning was spent cruising the Quad Cities, learning of the hangouts—Rock Island Brewing Company (RIBCO), TJ's, Lee's—and a few biker bars frequented by the

Grim Reapers Motorcycle Club. The fact that The Reapers had a chapter here spoke volumes. Those boys were notorious runners of drugs and weapons throughout the Midwest. Things could get interesting. Joey also told 'Roger' the names of two of the other big players in the area. Not as big as Harker and James, but who still had a sizeable market-share for their products-of-choice. And who were also supplying The James Gang with wholesale goods, for their own distribution network. Cooperative competitors. Coopetition, one might say.

Smoking pot was always a thing for the hip crowd, and the Quad Cities were no exception. It was never hard to find a dime bag or a lid—but that all came from someone else's pound or kilo. Those were, in the case of the Quad Cities, often supplied by 'The Brakeman.' The Brakeman—actually named Mike Downing—worked for the Rock Island Line Railroad. He actually was a brakeman. According to Joey, Downing would come home from his railroad trips carrying a duffle bag filled with very high-quality dope. He would then spend hours at his kitchen table, .44 magnum at his side, sifting out all the stems and seeds. He had a reputation for selling the best product on the market. He was very popular. And, since the Fort Ord bust had all but stopped the inflow through their military connections, he was the principal supplier to Cody and Gary—

The James Gang. His product was the 'preferred choice' of those with the bucks to pay the premium price. Gary and Cody had that set of customers.

The other player was known as Rocky. Rocky was a purveyor of coke and angel dust—PCP. As Joey explained, Rocky, too, had very high-quality goods in plentiful supply. No one was sure where he got his stuff, but he always delivered. Like Mike Downing, Rocky had filled the supply line gap for Cody and Gary after theirs was interrupted. Rocky was known to be a Nam Vet, like so many others of his age. He never spoke much about it, but Joey was an observant fellow.

"Rocky wears a Yard Bracelet," he told Roger/Rob.

'Yard' was the slang name given to the Montagnard's—indigenous peoples of the Central Highlands in Vietnam. During the war, they worked closely with the South Vietnamese and the US Army. Particularly with the US Special Forces. They were known to give the gift of a brass bracelet to those soldiers that they trusted and worked alongside. If Rocky had such a bracelet, he likely also had skills, similar to Rob's own. That called for a very special degree of consideration.

"Which one do you want to meet first?" Asked Joey.

"Neither."

"Neither?"

"That's right," Rob said, "neither. I don't even want them to know I'm in town. I have other ideas." He wanted them out of circulation, but not after just having met 'some dude from not around here.' No sense spooking the herd. "Like the older bull said, in the old joke…let's walk down there, and fuck them all!"

Chapter 5—Eliminating the Competition

Rob spent the next couple of weeks getting his cover established. Working with the Task Force, he had secured a fine rental house—just fancy enough to show that he had some means, but not too over-the-top—on a couple of acres of Rock River riverfront. No prying neighbors—and no easy way to be followed home. He spent the nights going to the clubs and bars with Joey and his rather attractive entourage. Man, it would be so damned easy to violate at least one rule of engagement—no fraternizing—or carnal knowledge—of the enemy. But he could still come close… had to keep up the cover, after all. As Roger Lee, Rob knew he would be offered the occasional hit off a joint—easy to fake that—and the occasional line or spoon of coke. The coke was always a challenge for any undercover cop. Until some enterprising nerd at the DEA Training Center came up with the "tooter." This was a silver tube that also contained a filter. It allowed the agent to snort the coke, because the filter trapped it in the tube. Rob wore one of those gadgets around his neck, on a silver chain. That adornment also signaled that he was into the drug—always an advantage. In case a dealer insisted on using his own tooter, or a rolled-up bill, a bit of slight-of-hand was used—like using one hand to 'protect' the coke, by cupping it around the line, while discretely sweeping it ahead of the tooter with the little finger of the other hand. Risky, but so far, so good. The preferred approach was simply to always say something like, 'I'm in it for the business, not the buzz,' or, 'I don't shit where I eat.' In other words, avoid having to do any of the undercover magic tricks whenever possible.

During the days, Rob worked with the Task Force on other things, too—like taking down The Brakeman and Rocky. The first would be the easiest. A few discrete inquiries resulted in getting hands on Mike Downing's work schedules for the next few weeks. According to Joey's information, it was the southern trips that seemed to be where Downing got his bundles. One of those was on the schedule for the third day of the rotation. St. Louis, to be exact. The Task Force arranged for a surprise inspection of the train, which resulted in the arrest in Cape Girardeau, of one Michael Downing, a brakeman on the Rock Island Line. Terrible luck, that.

That bust left a gap in the local market. Sure, there was still plenty of pot to be had, but not the quality that The Brakeman offered. And that was exactly the plan.

Rocky would be a more unique problem. Rob Anderson would have preferred to go straight at him, even if it meant a violent confrontation. Which it probably would have. Rocky—real name Dean Rockland—had indeed been a Green Beanie, in Nam. And that, to Rob, was a problem. Rocky was a disgrace to the institution that Rob held so dear. Nothing closer than the SpecOps community. Death Before Dishonor, and all that. Facilitating the 'Death' part seemed appropriate, and Rob was more than willing to accommodate. That, however, did not work with the Master Plan. Rocky needed to be quietly taken out of circulation. Nothing suspicious, just MIA.

Joey, knowing folks who know folks, had provided good intel. Once every couple of weeks, Rocky would mount up his Harley for a road trip. No one knew much more than that. Not even the Task Force tails had been able to track him through the back roads of Illinois. But when he returned, he brought illegal smiles to a lot of local faces. Joey's sources didn't know where he was going, but they knew when he was going to visit his family in Indiana on the way back. That's all the info Rob needed. The Task Force knew that his family lived in Valparaiso, Indiana, about 200 miles from the Quad Cities. They planned to take Rocky down, right there at Mom's house. For this one, Rob wanted a piece of the action. It was personal. He wound up the 350 cubic inch V-8 in his Z-28 Camaro and made the run in two and a half hours.

When Rocky arrived at his parents' farm, outside of Valparaiso, his first hug was from a DEA Agent—Rob Anderson. Not a hug, really. A sliding front kick to the solar plexus. Rob was waiting behind a large oak tree, stepping out just as Rocky dismounted his machine. As Rocky lay on the ground, trying to catch his breath, Rob leaned over him so that his face was an inch away.

Through clinched teeth, Rob said, "Sua Sponte, motherfucker." Sua Sponte—the Ranger motto, meaning 'Of Their Own Accord.' The motto refers to the voluntary commitment required of each man that becomes a Ranger—which Rocky had done prior to qualifying for Special Forces. "You chose this road of your own accord, smearing the reputation of every Special Operations soldier. Now, this old Ranger is taking your ass down. Payback is a bitch, bitch!" Turning to the lead DEA Agent, Rob said, "Miranda his punk ass."

Rocky's saddlebags were filled with ten kilos of Peruvian rock cocaine. That ensured that his next visit with family would be through a glass window in a jailhouse visiting room. Interstate transportation and intent to distribute. This boy was going to have plenty of time to catch up on his reading in Club Fed.

On his ride back across Illinois, Rob began playing out next steps in his mind. These two busts would leave Gary Harker and Cody James with a bit of a supply issue. A gap which 'Roger' was setting himself up to fill. 'Take the Long Way Home' blared from his 8 track. Not tonight, Supertramp, not tonight. Rob had work to do.

Chapter 6—Penetrate and Radiate

The next morning, Rob reached out to Joey. Well, technically 'Roger' reached out, but whatever. They met for lunch at Adolf's, a popular taco joint. Rob made a point of getting there a bit early. He always did. It helped to keep things as much under control as he could hope to keep them. Joey strolled in, passing out smiles and nods and a howdy to pretty much everyone in the place. He was well known, and quite popular. Exactly why they had chosen this particular spot. Word would get around that there was a new dude in town—and he was good buds with Joey Hill. Solid credibility—they say you can't buy it. Rob knew better.

"I think this area is having an acute supply chain problem," said the Agent, sipping his lemonade, "time for you to help fill in the void."

"I can dig that, man. What's the plan?"

"I'd like to throw a very selective party, at my new digs. You're the party planner, if you get my drift." Rob was into his second taco. Damn tasty, too. "I need you to get the word to The James Gang that I have the product they need. Good shit—the best. Main channel, direct to the boys in California that were supplying their sources at the Arsenal." In fact, Roger Lee had been in that inner ring. Right until he was busted and spirited away into the system. If Cody and Gary knew any of the other major players well enough to call them, they would think Roger had gone rogue, but they would probably confirm his rep. If they knew any of the major players—which was unlikely. Folks don't like to give away their sources. Poor business practices. Or so Rob hoped.

The plan was simple enough—the Task Force would supply Rob with a significant stash of pot, ludes, coke and cash to be used as bait. Then, they would throw one helluva party—New Year's Eve seemed like a suitable date—at which the invitees could buy the drugs, in quantity. A carefully curated "guest list" would be the key—and it would include Gary Harker and Cody James. Then—WHAM!—the tried-and-true reverse sting.

In a 'reverse sting,' cops posing as drug dealers use a CI to lure potential buyers to come to a meeting, with wads of cash, from pockets to suitcases full, to buy drugs from the undercover cops. If the reverse sting was successful, the buyer would be handed the drugs, relieved of his cash, and busted. He'd be charged with Possession, Conspiracy to Possess, and Possession with Intent to Distribute—charges that carried a potential of many decades in prison if convicted. The cash would go into the coffers of the Agency or Department that ran the sting, and the

CI would receive a large cash award, usually based upon the amount of assets seized and/or the media value—headlines—the case garnered. Everyone comes out happy... except the perps, of course. The trick is it can't really be a one-off transaction. If a court determined that the buyer had no previous disposition to actually buy and distribute drugs, they might very well call the sting entrapment, throwing the whole thing to the curb. To avoid that, Rob always liked to make at least three buys from his targets—just to develop the pattern.

"Joey," the one called Roger spoke into the hotel phone, "I think we need to get out and mingle a bit."

"I'm up for that, man. Couple of good bands gigging around town, which means some hot after-parties. Dress for success!"

Joey picked up the DEA Agent at 9:00PM. On the way out of his room, Roger did a comms check with his Task Force tail, ensuring that he was well-covered. All systems go. Joey had arranged to meet some of the local drug illuminati at a club called TJ's—he knew the guys in the band, and there was always a house party after the gig.

The club did not disappoint. Hot babes, loud music—and more than a few patrons with that telltale cocaine gleam in their eyes. Joey nodded to a table against the wall to the right of the stage.

"You wanted to meet Gary and Cody—well, there they sit."

Gary was model-quality handsome. Shoulder-length dirty blonde hair, well-trimmed mustache, hip threads. Cody, not so much. He was a tall, strong looking dude, with a gunslinger-style western hat, dingo boots and a suede jacket with 8 inches of fringe hanging from the chest, bottom and sleeves. Classic outlaw look… even if it seemed like he was trying a tad too hard.

Leaning in, Joey said, "You can be sure that Cody is packing. He has a thing for his .38 revolver—never leaves home without it."

"How about an introduction?" Roger asked. No sense dragging things out. He'd already been in town for almost a month and was becoming accepted as a pal of Joey Hill, with lots of cash and some solid connections.

"Sure, but wait until the end of this set," the CI replied, "we can have a more personal conversation."

As the band wound down to take a "pause for the cause," the Agent and his CI casually made their way to the James Gang table.

"Yo, boys!" Joey's infectious smile always got one in return. Well, he got one back from Gary. Cody didn't seem like much of a smiley guy. "I want y'all to meet my pal Roger Lee. We go back to the Nam together!"

Gary motioned to sit. "Any friend of Joey's, and all that crap," he said, "where you from?"

"California," Rob/Roger lied, "out near Salinas. Got out of the Suck at Ft. Ord and just dug the area, so I hung around."

"What the fuck brings you to the Quad Shitties, man?" asked Cody, staring hard into Rob's eyes.

Maintaining solid eye contact with Cody, Rob answered, "Business, of sorts. Seems one of our distribution channels has had some supply chain issues. I'm here to sort out some of that." Rob finished with just the slightest hint of a humorless smile.

"Hmm," mused Gary, "what kind of 'distribution'?"

"Agricultural, you might say. Primarily distributed to the military. But, hey, I came out to enjoy the nightlife, man, not talk business—this is a righteous band!" Rob saw the poorly disguised concern in Gary's eyes.

Cody was still staring, with a none-to-trusting focus. Without breaking eye contact, he produced a small vial of white powder from his pocket. "I'm sure you have no problems with joining us in a line of some fine Peruvian, right? Straight off a rock the size of a marble." With this, he dumped out a health pile of the stuff, right there on the glass tabletop, dragging it into four lines, with the edge of a prodigious Buck knife.

"Yo, brother, is this even cool, right here?" asked Rob, with a couple of quick side glances. No one seemed to pay even a small bit of attention to their table.

"Fear not, man," spoke Joey, "this place is cool. Nobody gives a shit—and nobody fucks with the fellers!"

"After you, amigo," Cody watched him with an apprehensive glare.

"My pleasure, partner!" the man known as Roger replied, pulling the chain holding the silver tooter from his shirt, "It has been a long day." Rob bent over the table and drew one of the lines into the filtered device. Leaning back in his chair, he pinched his nostril shut and appropriately displayed the facial expression of a guy who had just blasted his sinuses with potent cocaine. He'd studied this move. Trained for it. Executed it successfully, many, many times. "Daaaamn," was all he said.

The three other men just laughed. "That's what I'm talkin' about!" Gary said, as he leaned into the table for his turn, followed by Joey and Cody.

The ice, so to speak, was broken.

"Roger here is cool, boys," spoke Joey. "We got a lot of things in common. Roger and his partners had been providing a steady supply of various goodies to our pal at the Arsenal. Or was until they transferred the good Captain. Y'all should probably have a chat about agriculture, ya know?" That wink. That smile.

"Gotta love this guy," thought Rob.

Rob spoke next, "Yeah, but not tonight. Tonight, I'm looking to score, not sell. Anyone seen Rocky—I paid the dude for an OZ of nose candy—ain't seen him since."

Joey looked up. "I saw him two days ago. He said he was 'going for a cruise,' which usually means one of his supply runs. Fear not, he's a reliable dude, he won't burn you!"

"How about an eight ball to hold you over?" Rob was surprised to hear Cody offer this up. Seems like he took the bait.

"That works. You have some fine ass shit right here. Happy to do business with you. I'm sure I'll be able to return the favor, in the not too distant future!" Rob reached for his wallet. "Do you take Diner's Club?" He asked, with a grin.

"Funny dude," laughed Gary, "we can settle up tomorrow. Joey knows how to reach us. $500 bucks."

Cody handed over a small bag—a corner of a baggie—holding the product.

Score one for the Good Guys, thought Rob, as he kicked back to focus on the band's next set… and to admire the local talent. This life does not always suck.

Chapter 7—Task Force Clean Sweep

The next week, leading into the Thanksgiving Holidays, was spent with Joey, setting up medium-sized buys, with other local and regional dealers. Rob was racking up plenty of evidence on a lot of mid-level players in the regional drug scene. The only ones even close to the volume of The James Gang was the Grim Reapers Motorcycle Club. They were also being targeted by the Task Force, but not by Rob. He didn't fit the profile… this time. That effort was being led by an Agent of the Illinois Bureau of Investigation, named Bobby Spragg.

Bobby surely did fit the profile. He'd infiltrated the Reapers almost ten years ago, after they were hired for "security" at a rock festival called Kickapoo Creek. He'd finally made his way through the ranks to become a trusted soldier, and part of the inner circle of the club's president. If ever there was hard duty, Bobby's job was the definitive example. He was one of a very few Agents in any organized law enforcement group to have free rein to do just about anything, short of outright murder. Bobby Spragg was also the lead State Agent on Inter-Agency Task Force Clean Sweep.

Clean Sweep was to be the culmination of years of investigative work, closing down much of the drug trafficking in the region, from Chicago to Omaha to Minneapolis to St. Louis. There had been some successes, but after the huge Fort Ord bust, the dots got connected. The supply chain was running with military precision—because military logistics specialists set it up! Rob's military history and his involvement in the California bust made him a natural for his role in Clean Sweep. And he was a fresh face, with a hip attitude. He and Bobby could not appear more different—and they hit it off immediately. Both Nam Vets. Both martial arts experts, both with a 'go fuck yourself' attitude when it came to incompetence. Both fully understanding that one wrong word or move could mean the end of the line. Both fully invested in Task Force Clean Sweep.

The other members of Clean Sweep were seasoned operators from different State Agencies. Local involvement was on a very selective basis. Local cops all had histories—college, high school, sometimes even grade school, with some of the very people they would have to take down. For Bobby and Rob, that posed too much risk. They would call the local yokels when they needed the cavalry, but the bloody tip of the spear consisted of non-local folks who worked their way into the underground world, slowly and methodically. There were, of course, a couple of guys like Joey Hill included. The Confidential Informants. But even those folks weren't fully in the fold. Not exactly the most stellar example of 'trustworthy' after all. Kept on a tight leash, they only interacted with their handlers, not made aware of the other Task Force agents. Effective. Important. Expendable.

"How's that asshole Joey treating you, bro?" Bobby had such a way with words. "I've never liked nor trusted the little prick."

"He's ok," Rob replied, with a grin. "I've pointedly clarified that he's gonna get hurt if he screws me over. So far, he's bringing his A Game."

"Watch your six. And don't underestimate him. I've witnessed his skills with that Korean excuse for a martial art—he's good and he's quick. If I recall, you also train in one of those karate wannabe systems, right? Couldn't find a real sensei?"

At this, Rob laughed out loud. He knew Bobby was quite proficient in KaJuKempo—itself, a hybrid mutt of a system, from Hawaii—Karate, Judo, Kempo. "Look who's calling the kettle black! Your Hawaiian dance moves ain't exactly 'old skool,' dude." Still, Rob had heard the tales of Bobby, dealing with a group of 1%'ers. If the shit came down, he wanted Bobby at his side.

"Just bustin' your chops, amigo," Spragg said, "I've read your packet. You were in some serious shit, back in the Bush. Glad to have you on our team!"

"Wanna hear my hair-brained plan?" asked Rob. "If it turns out as effective as it should be fun, we will have a great New Year's Eve!"

Rob laid out the scheme. The Task Force was to provide a van full of assorted product, to use in the reverse sting operation. Rob explained he wanted to throw a killer New Year's Eve party—fully catered, a band, the whole enchilada. Rob, Bobby and other members of Task Force Clean Sweep would invite their strategic targets to the bash—be there or be square. They would arrange for a series of 'clients,' to come out to the secluded house Rob was living in, to buy quantities of the best shit in the country. At midnight, the actual surprise would come down—a mass bust of every attendee! The important thing was for any invited 'guest,' to have sold drugs to an agent on at least three prior occasions. Can't have them crying entrapment, after all.

Bobby Spragg looked at Rob with a serious expression and said, "We've taken a poll and have unanimously decided that you are fucking insane. We also love this idea!"

"Agreed and agreed!" Rob stifled a laugh. "But now, what else do we have? How's the tail on my two favorite future defendants?" Rob hadn't seen either of the James Gang members since that night in the club.

Lieutenant Peggy Beck spoke up, "Three days ago, the guys took a flight out of O'Hare, to Frisco—in First Class. Our team there pick up on them and followed them but lost them north of the Golden Gate Bridge. They haven't been home since." Peggy was good. She'd been in the Illinois State Police for over a decade. She was perfect for undercover ops. Hip, fit, attractive, but not so dazzling that it intimidated other chicks. But sexy enough that she could play most guys to the hilt. She had become friends with Harker's wife. She was very close to the action, without appearing to be pushing things too hard.

"Another thing," chimed in Spragg, "that shit you bought from them? It was not street stuff. It's close to 95% pure. That means that they still have sources for excellent product, even after we took down the military connection. That's not good. Makes me even more curious about their California vacation."

Rob winced. "If they're still connected in the Bay Area, we could have problems. We hurt the network around Fort Ord, but we can be sure we didn't kill it. Roger Lee—aka 'Yours Truly,' could get blown."

"Ord is south of Frisco, right?" asked Bobby. "These dudes went north. How wide was the network?"

"Wide. While the shit we uncovered was coming up through the Panama Canal Zone as Army mail, we know there were other routes. Along with planes, trains and trucks, we suspected boats up from Mexico—fast speed boats—into some of the high-end beach towns, up near Bolinas—about 30 miles north of San Fran. From there, our friend in the base logistics office distributed to their buddies, on bases all over the country. We snatched Roger Lee out of that civilian loop. If our boys from Illinois moved up the chain to deal directly with their supplier's supplier, they will probably ask about Roger. My description matches, but if the lead dogs out there think Roger has gone rogue, trying to carve out his own niche from their territory, somebody's gonna get pissed."

"Last thing," said Bobby, "we can't hold Rocky forever. He is not willing to roll over. If we bust him loose, you might have some 'splainin' to do."

"Fuck." Seemed like all there was to say about that. "Figure something out, pronto!"

# # #

Their non-stop flight out of Chicago was a few minutes late, but that didn't worry the two hippie-looking Midwesterners. They had intentionally come in a day early for their meetings with the man in Bolinas. Planning for this trip had been under way for two weeks, and this was part of that plan.

"We'll use my fake license for the car and yours for the van," Gary Harker said to his partner. "You ready to do this thing?"

"I'm with you, man," came the reply from Cody James. "I've already reserved a U-Haul in Marin City. We can leave the car in a truck stop parking lot, up on Route 1."

This was going to be their biggest haul ever. Twenty kilos of fine Bolivian snow. More importantly, if their plan went right, they would put themselves in a position of power with their main supplier—even if that supplier wasn't pleased about it—a position that would get them better pricing on the best product, along with exclusive rights to supply every dealer from Denver to Chicago and Minneapolis to Kansas City.

The two would-be drug lords crossed Golden Gate Bridge, with FM radio station KSAN's Jive95 Radio Show playing Hot

Tuna's 'Keep on Truckin' at full volume. Harker rolled a joint from the baggie of pot he carried in his Dingo boot.

"Man, we are about to be fucking kings!" shouted Cody, giving his partner a high five.

"Yeah, baby!" Gary Harker was as excited as Cody James. "The shit is about to get real!"

"So," Cody said, exhaling a cloud of sweet Michoacan smoke, "let's go over the plan. First, we get the U-Haul van in Marin; I'll follow you in the van to that truck stop on Route 1, where we can scope out the parking lot, grab a bite of food and pick up some disposable cameras; then I'll follow you in the van up to Bolinas, where we can get a room at that cool old hotel in town."

"Right on," chimed in Gary. "we call Flores from there, arranging to come out to his place tomorrow morning. We leave the van at the hotel, so that we don't look like a couple of dweebs, rolling into his estate in a freakin' rental van." Gary couldn't help but laugh at the mental image of that. "Once up at his place, and after all the glad-handing and social bullshit, we casually start taking a few pictures of the 'scenery,' getting him in as many of them as we can get away with."

"Yep. Play the 'oh, wow, this is so cool!' bullshit to the hilt. He already thinks of us as a couple of harmless hillbillies. We can use that. He was pretty cool with us, the last two trips. No reason to think he won't be, this time." Cody was nicely buzzed, now. He continued, "Once we're back home with the product, the pictures will become our tickets to the high ground!"

The two friends did their planned business in Marin, drove to Smiley's Schooner Saloon and Hotel in Bolinas, checked in, then called their supplier.

"Yo, Rudolfo, Cody here. We are in town, brother. What's the plan for our meet-up?" James tried to keep the excitement out of his voice.

"Amigo! *Bienvenidos a Bolinas!*" Rudolfo Flores liked the two young dealers from Illinois. They were making him plenty of money, even after the Army connections had been broken. "You guys should come to the house for breakfast—I have a few special guests staying here, but it's still cool. I know you guys well enough. Just give them their space. Believe me, these guys are heavyweights. Definitely better if you don' try to get to know them. Let me just say this—we are all about to get a serious upgrade. I'll tell you more, tomorrow."

"Perfect," Cody replied, "hey man, would it be cool if we take a few snapshots of your house and docks and shit? Folks back home have seen nothing like this, that's for sure."

"As long as no people are in them, man. But, hey, you already knew that, right? See you boys tomorrow."

Cody gave Gary a thumbs-up. "We're cool, man! We need to use up a couple of the cameras on landscapes and boats and shit, just to cover our asses. We also need to be sure to find a way to get Flores and maybe his 'special guests' in at least a few of the pictures. Gotta be cool about that, though. We don't want to blow this before we ever get started!"

Cody and Gary arrived at the luxurious seaside estate of Rudolfo Flores, at around 8:30 AM, in time for a wonderful breakfast. The views were magnificent, looking over the Pacific Ocean. Rudolfo sat with them for a few minutes, then excused himself to join the other guests at a table across the expansive patio.

Three Latin-looking men and one Caucasian man sat at the other table. The white guy gestured towards the two hippies, obviously not excited by their presence. Rudolfo seemed to placate the man, then sat down. The men were having a very animated discussion. Cody and Gary finished their breakfast, waved to Rudolfo, then walked to the edge of the patio and began taking snapshots of the amazing vista. Cody turned back to face the house and snapped a few more shots—several of which happened to include the table full of men, still engrossed in their conversation.

Just after noon, Rudolfo reconnected with the two dealers from Illinois.

"Gentlemen," Flores began, "I'm sorry for the delay." He added, in a low voice, "These guys are helping us to get a much better quality of product, at much better prices. Their connections are almost unbelievable!"

"I'm going to send you home with some of the new stuff. Same deal—you have thirty days to pay me for what you take. Believe me, you won't have any trouble selling it. Twenty keys, right?"

"Wow, man, that all sounds amazing! But hey, who the fuck are these guys? I thought you were already at the top of the pyramid, man," Gary was probing.

"I can't tell you who they are, but the gringo flew in from New Orleans—that's where a lot of product hits the States. That's all you need to know. And believe me—all you WANT to know" Flores glanced over his shoulder. "Another thing, "he said, "they are freaking out over you guys taking pictures. They want me to take the cameras from you. *Lo siento*, boys. Buy some postcards at the hotel or something."

"All good, brother," Cody had planned for this possibility, "I'll leave them on the table. We will bring our van to the boathouse tomorrow morning. Assuming that's still where we'll do the pick-up?"

"*Bueno*," Flores replied, and yes, at the boathouse, as usual. See you *mañana*."

"By the way, Rudolfo," Cody spoke, "you ever know a dude from out here, name of Roger Lee? He says he was involved in the Army thing."

"I know of him, sure," Flores replied, "haven't seen him for quite a while. Why do you ask?"

"He's out where we live. Said he's picking up the distribution from where our military connection left off. Figured you might have a line on him," Gary said.

"He knows his stuff, but I'm not pleased that he's sticking his nose in our business," Flores looked annoyed. "I'll do some digging."

Gary Harker and Cody James stood, shook hands with Roberto Flores, waved politely at the group of men standing on the manicured lawn, then placed their disposable cameras on the patio table. Except for the camera which held the images of the group of men, enjoying coffee and conversation, overlooking the ocean and cliffs of beautiful Bolinas, California.

A decision they would come to regret.

Gary followed Cody and the U-Haul van to the boathouse, the next morning. They convoyed to the truck stop outside of Marin, then took the long drive back to Illinois, quite pleased with themselves.

Chapter 8— 'Tis the Season

The Task Force filled the next few weeks with planning—and buying, of course. Because of the interstate transportation and Federal conspiracy charges, Rocky and Mike Downing were still in the lockup, as 'Material Witnesses.' They can hold a material witness as long as necessary to "prevent a failure of justice." This means that the people being brought in under material witness warrants can be detained for as long as a judge deems it necessary. One reason to hold material witnesses is that they may be likely to flee the country… or compromise a major drug interdiction case. Like this one.

One problem did crop up, however. A big problem. Cody and Gary had been avoiding 'Roger' ever since their return from California weeks ago. The concern was that they had been provided some direct information about Roger, that made them skittish. Rob's back channels to the DEA teams in the Bay Area had no scuttlebutt that made them think his cover had been blown, but something was definitely up. Rob had Joey come by the rental house. It was December 23rd—no time to have all this fall apart now.

"What's the word, man?" Rob was direct, as usual.

"Well, you know the guys are back, and they are reportedly working on a pretty big deal. They haven't been all that friendly to me, either. But I don't think they know you're a cop." No grin on Joey's face today.

"Yeah," Rob took a drink of his coffee, "Peggy Beck hasn't felt that either. She says Gary's wife told her he made some comment about 'Roger' being a dangerous guy to do business with. I can only surmise that their Cali contacts are pissed to learn that they are dealing with a former partner, whom they now see as a competitor. Still not cool for us."

"I'm still hoping to get them to the bash," Joey spoke, while refilling his own cup, "I'll play it like they should keep their enemies close. You get that, right?"

"I'm with you," though Rob wasn't sure he was, "let's hope it works."

"Won't be a walk in the park, but I think we can make it happen," Joey said. The twinkle was back. "They're, shall we say, 'intrigued' by you. Besides, Gary's old lady is like eight months pregnant—he sure ain't gettin' much at home. He knows I'll have some serious talent, at this blowout. If you'll pardon my choice of words."

Both guys cracked up, at that one. That was the last bit of humor that they would know, for a long time.

#   #   #

"Dude, it's time we made the call to Flores," Gary Harker said, between hits on a bong, "let's wish him a Merry Christmas!"

Cody James laughed. "Well, for us, it will be. Make the call."

The two drug-dealing friends were in Gary's woodworking shop. Gary picked up the phone and dialed the number of Rudolfo Flores, in Bolinas, California.

"*Hola, dígame,*" came the voice on the other end.

"*Feliz Navidad, amigo*, it's Gary Harker calling! I've got good news and bad news. Which do you want first?"

"I am not a fan of bad news, man. You'd better give me that first." Flores did not sound pleased.

"Well, Rudolfo, here's the deal. We aren't going to pay you for this last twenty kilos. In fact, we want twenty more and we want exclusive rights to all your product for the entire

Midwest." Gary waited for the other man to scream at him. It didn't come.

Calmly, Flores said, "I see. And in what fairy-tale world do you think that becomes a reality, *pendejo*?"

"Let's call it our Christmas wish," Gary said, "and you're like Santa Claus. Thing is though, we have not been good little boys. In fact, just the opposite. Remember those cameras we had out at your place? Well, there was one more. We have several very good, very clear pictures of you and your 'special guests.' As long as you work with us, they will never see the light of day. If you choose not to… well… do the math. I'm sure the DEA would be very interested in why a guy from New Orleans was in Bolinas, dealing with a Colombian coke supplier, don't you think? But wait, don't you want the good news?"

"No, motherfucker, there is no good news. You have just stepped into the deepest shit you've ever imagined. Nobody fucks with me. And threatening my friend from New Orleans is an even faster road to Hell. Now, let me tell you assholes exactly how things are going to go.

"First, do you think we would trust two low-level gangsters from halfway across the country, with all the stuff we've fronted, without some security in place? Don't you wonder how it is that you've not been busted already? Let me tell you, dumbass—we have a high-ranking cop on our payroll out there. A cop that you know well, yet never suspected was a cop. I know more about your business than you think. I also know all there is to know about your family and also your partner's ex-wife and two kids. And that should worry you both—very much so."

Gary Harker's blood turned to ice water. He hadn't expected this reaction. He and Cody knew Rodolfo Flores was a well-placed supplier, but thought he was a bit of wimp. Effeminate, even. Neither had expected the aggressive response they now heard.

"Two nights from now – Christmas night – I am personally going to come there to see you. I will not be alone. You will arrange to return all of my product, cash for any product that you've already sold, and, most importantly, each and every copy of these pictures you claim to have. If I am satisfied, your families will live to celebrate the beginning of the new decade." Flores' tone told Gary that this was not an idle threat. "Don't try to fuck with me," Flores continued, "I will know about it. Things will not go well for you. I will call you when I'm there, on this number. You will meet me when and where I tell you. Do not bring the cocaine to me – arrange a drop where my associates can pick it up. That way, I don't have to worry about you setting me up, which again would not go well for either of you. And we wouldn't enjoy hurting your pregnant wife, Gary. But trust me—we will hurt her. We will rape her, then we will cut that baby out of her, all in front of your other kids. Then, we will kill them all. You don't want that, do you?"

"Wait man, please, just wait. Can I call you back in twenty minutes? I need to talk to Cody and make some arrangements." Gary was on the verge of freaking out, and his voice was about to crack.

"Twenty minutes," Flores replied, "But, Gary, do not think this is a negotiation. It most definitely is not."

"We are truly fucked, brother." Gary was almost in tears. "I never thought it would go like this. I know you overheard the conversation, but man, I FELT the conversation. We need to do what he says. And who the fuck is this unknown narc he's talking about? I thought our shit was clear!"

"Jeezus, man, is he going to snuff us?" Cody was pale. "Do we have enough cash? What about the dope, man? We've already cut it once. We are screwed, Gary."

"I don't think he's going to kill us, bro, but we a definitely out of business," Gary didn't sound confident. "And the pictures. I thought they would be insurance. Man, were we wrong. Still, we will only take him two of the three sets of prints we made. We'll leave the other one with Mike Callow in an envelope. Tell him if anything happens to us, take them to the cops. At least maybe Flores will go down, too. We just have to do what we can to protect Marie and Patsy and the kids."

Twenty minutes later, Rudolfo got another call. This time, it was Cody James on the phone. Cody gave Flores the address of a body shop in Rock Island where, on Christmas night, the drugs would be waiting, concealed inside the air tank of a compressor. Flores abruptly ended the call.

#   #   #

The morning of December 26th, Rob got a call from Peggy Beck. She said that Harker's wife was freaking out, because Gary had left the evening before—Christmas—to make a delivery to a guy in Rock Island. He told her it was a compressor, and for whatever reason it was critical to do, right then. He hadn't come home. Peggy said that the Task Force tail had followed Gary and Cody, in Cody's black pickup, to an auto shop in Rock Island. They dropped off a piece of equipment, then left again. They meandered around for a while, then probably realizing they were being tailed, and managed to lose the shadow, somewhere outside of town on some farm roads. It was Christmas night—most of the regular team were given time off to spend with family. The tail was being handled by a couple of new guys, that weren't familiar with the area—that was now an obvious problem.

On December 30th, Harker's wife filed a Missing Person report with the Rock Island County Sheriff. Gary hadn't come home, or even called. Bobby Spragg had sent members of the Task Force to the auto shop to ask some questions and to get their hands on the 'compressor.' The owner, who lived next door, said that all he knew was that Cody and Gary had made arrangements with him to drop off the piece of equipment, and some 'other dude' had come by about an hour later, to get it. Conveniently, the shop owner had provided a weak description of the second man, and what he was driving. Dead end.

While it seemed obvious that Gary and Cody would not be in attendance at the Operation Clean Sweep New Year's Eve Party, Rob had definitely baited the hooks for many other medium to large-scale dealers in the area. It was game on, with or without the James Gang.

Chapter 9—The Party

In the months leading up to the New Year's Eve Sting, the Task Force undercover agents had made 163 individual buys from over 87 dealers, as they nestled their way into the social lives of their suspects. According to Bobby Spragg, this number was 'extraordinary.' Nothing on the records compared to this effort. Most of those dealers were scheduled to come by 'Roger's' house, well before the party, to buy some large quantities of pot and coke. Its discreet location at the end of a dirt track, the rental house was the perfect place to hold the reverse buys without the whole town finding out. As soon as they made the purchase and loaded it into their own vehicles, they would get the surprise of their lives—being rapidly victimized by the Reverse Buy Sting! Once the drugs had been loaded into a suspect's car, cops would jump out and arrest the dealer, impound their vehicle, take their money—*and* get the drugs back. God Bless America!

Soon, the party would begin. In preparation, some officers decorated the house with blue and white ribbons—police colors—a nice touch, if Rob said so himself. As the clock stuck midnight, they'd bust every fucking dealer with an outstanding warrant. But, not before having a bit of fun with them, first!

At about 3:00 p.m., the first car full of drug dealers arrived. Peggy Beck pointed her video camera out of the front window of the house and pressed record. It was just five hours before the party was to begin, and time was tight before the guests arrived. As suspects parked next to Rob's car, and Peggy zoomed in on Rob and Darin (another Task Force Member) as they opened the trunk. The dealer passed 'Roger' a shoebox filled with over $87,000 in cash. Rob and Darin then helped the dealers load the bales of weed into their car. Then Rob pulled his WWII-vintage Remington-Rand M1911 pistol. That was the sign.

"Go! Go! Go! Go!" yelled a gang of uniformed officers, appearing from nowhere. "Put your hands on the car!" they shouted.

One car after another drove into the trap, in 20-minute intervals. Rob and Darin pulled off three busts, confiscating over $100,000 in cash. They arrested the last buyer at around 6:30 p.m., just an hour and a half before the party.

"Get these fuckers out of here!" Rob shouted, "If the rest of these assholes see uniformed officers out there arresting people, man, they'll be gone in a New York minute!"

They bundled the arrested men into vans and kept them away from telephones to stop them from tipping off their associates.

Uniformed cops and Undercover cops jumped into their hiding places as 'party-guests'—aka 'suspects' began to arrive around 7:30 p.m. They were all clearly carrying guns, adding a whole new—but not unexpected—dimension to the evening. It was Bobby Spragg's idea to invite Tom Charnov, a photojournalist who posed as an event photographer. Bobby warned him to be ready to shoot a major police operation. The place filled up with thugs. The Task Force members could see the weapons under their sports jackets — then they began to get drunk on all the free liquor.

"What a great recipe for a shit-show," thought Rob / Roger. He invited each new arrival inside. He had also laid out bricks of marijuana inside the dining room, to raffle off for $100 per ticket. "Step on up, friends, ya pays yer dollar and ya takes yer chances!" No truer words could have been spoken.

The festivities began. The bad guys were quite impressed. It was clearly the coolest party of the year. The band announced itself as a weed-loving four piece whose name, SPOC, stood for

'Somebody Protect Our Crops.' In fact, it was COPS spelled backwards, and an undercover Rock Island police officer was the bandleader. The department had found him after making a request over police radio for any officers who could play instruments. Three other officers had also come forward to play guitars and drums. The band sucked, but alcohol and drugs make any band sound better—and any potential fuckbuddy more attractive.

The 'invited guests' downed pitchers of beer and cheered as SPOC dived into its first song. Around 9:00PM, another group of gangsters showed up—they were all tucking into the free food and drink. There were clearly some rivals in the crowd. The guys from the Reapers hung close together. Brothers from the West End hung out with some of their pals from St. Louis. Everybody was eyeballing everybody else, but there seemed to be a sort of detente in play. This was a good thing—a shootout between guests would be a not-so-good thing.

The place was shaping up to be a good representation of the Dr. Hook and the Medicine Show song, 'Freakin' at the Freaker's Ball':

> The FBI is dancin' with the junkies
> All the straights, swingin' with the funkies
> Across the floor and up the wall
> We're freakin' at the freaker's ball, y'all
> We're freakin' at the freaker's ball

From his hiding position, Darin ticked off suspects from the guest list as more cars arrived. Most had shown up, but a few had not. Including the main event—the James Gang. Neither Cody nor Gary had been seen nor heard from since Christmas evening.

As the night progressed, the criminals were watching the marijuana raffle prize with greedy eyes. A kilo of Michoacan pot for a hundred bucks—yeah, baby!

At 11:00, Rob / Roger stepped up to the mic. "Brothers and Sisters," he began, "cool news! Since several of my invited guests seemed to have made other plans for the evening," a loud 'Booo!' came up from the crowd, "it seems we have enough of the always wild, extra mild Michoacan marijuana for everyone!" A raucous cheer from the guests, this time. "Please proceed to the dining room to grab your brick—and try not to kill anyone, ok? And hey—please don't everyone fire up a joint inside—you'll set off the smoke alarms! Light up on the back deck but be back in here before midnight—this party is hot, but you ain't seen nothin' yet!" Rob knew that there was no way out of the back yard, unless someone trudged across the frozen Rock River—not too likely, in party shoes!

There was nothing but jovial laughter, high-fives, and slaps on the back, as the 75 guests filed into the dining room to claim their prize. Not surprisingly, a few did drift to deck for a joint or one-hitter, but at a balmy three-degrees, the weather wasn't all that inviting for most. They just brought their new stash back to their tables—right where the Task Force wanted them.

As midnight approached, the party was in full swing. Behind the scenes, though, it was pure tension: Sweaty hands gripped weapons. Synchronized watches were checked. As the clock moved to 11:50, the band knew it was time to give the signal to get on with the program. They played the pre-arranged signal song: 'I Fought the Law (and the Law Won).'

As the song ended—at the stroke of midnight, Rob jumped onto the stage and grabbed the mic, "Happy fucking New Year—now let's have some fun," he shouted. "Everybody here that's a cop, stand up!" The whole place broke out in laughter. Until they looked around the room.

A dozen undercover officers rose to their feet and a dozen more uniformed detectives burst through the door.

"Okay!" Rob yelled. "All the rest of you motherfuckers put your hands on the table because you're under arrest! This is a bust!"

Rob was standing on the elevated bandstand—about eight inches off the floor. He had a good view across and around the room. He heard and saw the laughter turn to disbelief, and a chorus of "What the fuck?" rising from the crowd. At a table nearest to the front, one soon-to-be-defendant quickly stood up, while reaching for something inside his jacket.

"You motherfucker!" the dude yelled, as he reached to his waist band. That's all he got out, before Rob hit him in the jaw with a jumping roundhouse kick, leaping from the band riser. The wise guy went down hard. As Rob landed, another of the guys at the table stood up. Rob spun, hitting him with an elbow strike to the face, followed by a sidekick to the solar plexus. Game, set and match.

'KACHUNK'—the sound of a dozen cops racking their 12-gauge shotguns punctuated Rob's next shouted command.

"All you assholes, FREEZE!" Nothing quite so emasculating as that very distinct sound. The assholes froze... and probably puckered up a bit, too.

There were close to forty busts that would result in charges. In most cases, their dates weren't arrested—most of the major players had warrants already issued, they popped others for possession. They all had at least a pound of newly acquired pot, after all. The Task Force expected that most, if not all, would try to pursue Entrapment Complaints. That's why the previous transactions were so important. As a Supreme Court case stated, 'Government agents may not implant in an innocent person's mind the disposition to commit a criminal act, but they can use artifice, stratagem, pretense or deceit.' If those last four words didn't sum up this bust, nothing could. That this operation took place on a Holiday meant the perps would get an extra couple of days in the cooler, prior to being arraigned. Life's a bitch, ain't it?

The Task Force was careful about keeping their in-place assets viable. Bobby Spragg, while at the location, was always out of sight. He was filming the whole thing, from discrete locations. Peggy Beck was the same—close enough to engage, if needed, but out of the mix. They corralled Joey Hill up with everyone else. Difference being, he wasn't arrested or taken to the clink.

Easy cover, because there were so many arrested that it took multiple vans and five different jails to hold them. Once the crooks were gone, Bobby, Peggy and Joey rejoined Rob and other members of the Task Force and assisting officers in the house.

"Well Bobby, what now?" asked Rob. His cover in this operation was blown wide open—as was the plan.

"Shit, brother," laughed Spragg, "all this food and free booze—let's have a fuckin' party!"

The group broke out in a fit of laughter and high fives. Why the hell not—it's New Year's!

Chapter 10—River City Blues

As expected, several of those arrested started trying to cut deals by offering up their own contacts. Flipped faster than fried eggs on a Waffle House grill. Shit was now rolling uphill, from Omaha to Chicago, to Minneapolis to St. Louis. A damn good dent in the Midwest drug market. Several of them implicated Gary Harker and Cody James. As a kicker, the local cops would benefit from over $200,000.00 in confiscated cash from the reverse sting buys. A nice influx into their crime-fighting budgets. But still no news on the whereabouts of Gary Harker and Cody James. Gary's pregnant wife had filed a Missing Person report and the Task Force had issued a region-wide BOLO. They issued warrants, based on the previous drug buy Rob had pulled off—a small charge, but enough to get them in handcuffs. If they could be found, that is.

Rob, of course, was now out in the open. He took part in search warrants at the homes of both Harker and James, and at Harker's woodworking shop. The shop was the last place they were, before delivering the 'compressor' to the auto shop in Rock Island. Both homes were clean, but the woodworking shop had some interesting tidbits. Along with the usual tools a craftsman might use, there was also an acetylene cutting torch, a welder and several empty cans of spray lacquer—for metal. More interesting were the empty boxes of quart sized sandwich bags, and several garbage bags of what looked like the wax-type paper used to wrap kilos of coke. Those wrappers had traces of what tested to be very pure cocaine residue. Other interesting discoveries included large bottles of Mannitol, a powdery laxative, known to be used for cutting cocaine, a triple-beam scale, and several large glass bowls, also containing residue. There was also a receipt from U-Haul, for a van rented in Mill Valley, California, on the same day the guys arrived in San Francisco, a few weeks back. It wasn't in either of their names, however.

Taken in context, the Task Force theorized that the James Gang had flown out, eluded the local tail assigned to follow them, then rented the van and probably ditched their rental car. The assumption was, they did their deal in Cali, then drove the goods home in the U-Haul van, though the local U-Haul offices had no record of a van being turned in anywhere in the area. Once back, the Task Force figured they broke down the kilos, then cut the coke to some value-enhancing ratio for distribution. Most of it, that is. The theory was that a bigger deal was in play. One that involved cutting open the air tank on a shop-sized compressor, filling the tank with a large quantity of the cocaine, re-welding the tank and re-painting it. That all seemed to fit neatly with the known facts. What was missing was the big thing: who took possession of the tank?

Rob and his new Task Force buddy Darin paid a visit to the owner of the auto shop, where the 'compressor' was dropped off, and where it was later picked up by 'some dude.' That story left more than a couple of questions. The owner had already been interviewed and given a statement, but Rob wanted more. He just couldn't quite buy the narrative.

"So, let's review," Rob looked hard into the shop owner's eyes, "James and Harker just randomly had you 'hold on' to a valuable piece of equipment, so that 'some other dude' could stop by and pick it up? That's your BS story, man? How well do you know those guys? You didn't think this was a weird thing to ask? On freakin' Christmas Day?"

The shop owner was clearly not the sharpest tool in the shed. He was also obviously quite buzzed for 10:30 in the morning. "Seriously, Officer, that was how it happened. Okay, I've known the guys for years. Cody used to help around here sometimes, and, well, I occasionally scored some shit from him. They gave me an eight ball of coke for just doing this thing for them. Good shit, too!" based on the look in the guy's eyes, Rob could see he was still enjoying some of that, almost two weeks later. "The other dude came about an hour later, driving a U-Haul van. I didn't know him, never seen him before. I helped him load the compressor and he split. That's all I got, man, I swear!"

"U-Haul van?" Rob repeated, watching pieces come together in his mind, "you told the local cops that you weren't sure what the guy was driving. Did you happen to notice the plates?" Rob knew the plates wouldn't mean anything—those vans get moved from place to place all the time.

"No, sir," came the reply. "I just wanted to get back out of the cold. And I didn't want anyone to mix me up in this—that's why I lied." Another dead end.

"In your statement, you gave a half-assed description of the 'other dude,'" Rob was drilling this speed freak with his stare, "what else can you tell us, besides 'a Chicago Bears hat, a gray coat and a dark mustache'?"

The shop owner was feeling the heat of Rob's stare. "Nothing, man, honest… wait…" the guy paused, "I'm sure he was a Latino. Had an accent, but not Mexican. Like that, but kinda different, ya know?" Considering the large Latino population of this part of the world, Rob found this information less than helpful, but it was at least something.

"So, you're a linguist? You can tell the difference between Latino accents? Impressive!" Rob added that last with as much sarcasm as he could muster, "you're a fucking genius!"

"Fuck you dude," Shop Guy said, "I dated a Mexican chick for five years. I know what the accent sounds like. This dude's accent was different."

Rob thanked the guy for his time, left him a card and told him to call if anything else came to mind. Busting him for lying to the first cops would be just too much paperwork.

Basically, they had bupkus, when it came to the James Gang, except for another dozen people ready to sell them down the Muddy Mississippi. It didn't seem likely to Rob, Bobby or other members of the Task Force, that Harker would just run out on his pregnant wife. The guy was a crook, sure, but no one thought he was that big of a prick. Cody has an ex and two kids, too. Just didn't fit the profile of either guy. That only left the option of them being disposed of, by parties unknown. Absolutely nothing had popped because of the BOLO. So, yeah, bupkus. Which sucked.

Rob had the blues. The only cure was… well… the blues. There was a great blues joint in Rock Island, called RIBCO—Rock Island Brewing Company. Rob had the need for some serious string bending electric blues, so took the night off to get a little loose. With his cover out the window, he needed a wingman, though. His first choice was Bobby Spragg—that would be a seriously good time—but nope, Bobby was still deep under with the Reapers.

"Yo, Darin," Rob called across the squad room. They were working out of the Rock Island County Sheriff's Office. "You into the blues?"

"My musical tastes are expansive," Darin replied, "I like both kinds—country and western!"

"A dyed in the wool shit kicker," thought Rob. Out loud he said, "well, dust off your boots and come with me tonight, for a proper indoctrination to some proper music. I'll meet you at Jim's Rib Haven at 7:00. We can stuff our faces, then go check out this guitar player I've been hearing about. A kid named David Nicholson." He'd been eager to try Jim's—all the locals raved about the food. And this kid, David, was supposedly an uncanny blues guitarist. He had a harp player in the band, who went by the name 'Buffalo.' Nothing but the highest praise from the most reliable sources—a bunch of low-life druggies, who lived for the blues. This job did come with a few unique perks, after all. The band was named River City Blues.

Jim's Rib Haven did not disappoint. Rob was pretty sure he had never had ribs that good. Cool, down-home vibe to the place, too. He and Darin finished off a rack each, plus fries and beans. Definitely a good prelude to the blues! They got to RIBCO around the time the first set was starting. The guitar player looked like he was about 15 years old, but man, he could play! The harp player, Buffalo, was a skinny white dude with an afro, who clearly knew his way around the briefcase full of harmonicas he had in a stand on the stage. He also shared in the vocals, which weren't too shabby at all. The bass and drums were right in the pocket. Two shots of Cuervo and a cold beer later, the two cops were feeling the music. Until the shit-show started.

"Hey, motherfucker," the voice came from behind Rob, at the bar, "ain't you the fuckin' narc that just took a bunch of my brothers down?"

Rob had taken the precaution of cutting his hair to a professional length, had trimmed his bodacious 'stache and was wearing fake glasses—but that was seemingly not quite enough.

"Dude, you got the wrong guy," he said, turning half on to the guy, in a solid ready position. Darin, who was just returning from the head, took up a position that covered Rob's. "Lemme buy you a beer."

"Fuck that, cop! Your ass is mine tonight!"

The gentleman was a few inches taller that Rob's six feet and weighed a couple dozen pounds more. He also had two pals with him, of similar dimensions. The loudmouth was wearing a pair of classic bib overalls, and looked every bit the duffus Iowa farm boy. He reached his left hand out to grab Rob's jacket lapel, while drawing his right back for a haymaker. As he did so, Anderson took a sliding step forward, grabbing the straps on the fellow's bibs in both hands, then jerked on them as he launched a headbutt into the big boy's face. The momentum of the assailant's weight coming forward with his punch, assisted by Rob's pull, was halted by a force equal to being hit in the face with an eight-pound bowling ball. The guy went to his knees, with Rob keeping his grip on the bib-straps, ready for a follow up strike. Which wasn't required. Physics: not just a good idea; it's the law.

The other two guys were taken aback by what had just happened to Farm Boy, but that didn't last long. As they prepared to launch at Rob, Darin stepped in and simultaneously kicked the lead guy on the outside of his left knee, while pulling his badge and gun and yelling "Police, motherfuckers, freeze!" Even over the strains of the Alman Brothers song, 'One Way Out,' the pop of the broken knee was loud. The screamed command brought the music to a stop. So much for a relaxing night of blues music.

It only took a second for the bouncers to get into the mix. They secured the offending idiots, saying that they'd already called the police. Rob told them to just let it slide. No need for the paperwork on anyone's part. These redneck druggies weren't worth the hassle.

"Tell RIPD that we aren't pressing charges," said Rob, showing the head bouncer his DEA shield, "send these pukes to the hospital." River City Blues kicked off a solid rendition of George Thorogood's 'Bad to the Bone.' An appropriate note on which to end the evening.

Chapter 11—Onward and Upward

By the end of February 1980, all the legal machinations were well underway. Indictments, arraignments, a couple of plea deals, and at least two new members of the Witness Protection Relocation Club, including our pal, Joey. In his case, the story was put out that he had skipped out on his bond and had been killed in a shootout with a State Trooper in South Carolina. In fact, Joey was living the good life in Zihuantanejo, with a new identity. And still nothing surfacing about Harker and James.

Rob Anderson was being reassigned to the DEA Training Facility in downtown Washington, DC. He assumed that his field days were soon to be behind him. A good thing, he figured—he was getting a bit long in the tooth for the undercover drug interdiction racket. Time to move on. He had plenty to teach the Young Turks coming into the game, and he was also becoming more interested in the "business side" of the drug trade. Following the money. He had applied and been accepted into a Master of Business Administration program at Georgetown University—fully paid for by Uncle Sam, of course. Though he was leaving the field on a high note, he remained frustrated by losing The James Gang. Such a comedy of errors it took to let them slip away. That was another good reason to move on—the idiocy was getting to him. Rob had another seven years before his twenty was up. He planned to use those years to develop skills and education that would be more transferrable to the 'real world' of civilian life.

A few days before his planned departure, Bobby Spragg contacted him. Bobby had kept clear of Rob since the New Year's Eve bust. Couldn't risk any cracks in his own cover.

"Hey, amigo, can't let you get way without tossing back a few rounds," Booby said through the phone, "we have this out of the way joint out in Geneseo, where we can meet safely. Peggy, Darin and a few of the other Operation Clean Sweep Task Force members will be there. I'm sure it won't be as good as your last party, though," both men broke out in a hearty laugh, "but I doubt anyone will go to jail! Tomorrow night, at Ray's Place."

"See you guys there," answered Anderson, "and don't expect the Feds to pay the fucking tab!"

It was a delightful party. Everyone was upbeat and feeling good about everything except losing James and Harker—and Rob's departure, of course. Still, spirits were high, they filled the jukebox with great tunes, the beer was cold, and the fried chicken was out of sight! A pleasant way to end an assignment.

The next morning, Rob loaded up the Z-28, wondered how long they'd let him keep this cool ride, and headed east on Interstate 74.

Rob checked in to the Marriott Hotel, near the location of the Drug Enforcement Administration Training Facility, on March 15th, 1980. Within two weeks, he had secured an apartment in Georgetown, near the University. That's where Rob Anderson would stay, for the rest of his service with the DEA—or so he thought. He was fully enrolled and eager to begin the spring semester at the school, and to get active in the new training programs for incoming agents at the Facility. It was an exciting time to be part of the DEA and Rob was coming in as a bit of a rock star.

In April 1975, DEA had created the first of its central tactical units (CENTAC) to concentrate enforcement efforts against major drug trafficking organizations. Prior to this, due to lack of coordination on a national level, they terminated many drug investigations following the arrest of low-level dealers or an occasional top figure—who often was quickly replaced. However, CENTAC targeted major worldwide drug trafficking syndicates from a central, quick-response command post in Washington, D.C. Eight CENTACs investigated heroin manufacturing organizations in Lebanon, Asia and Mexico.

Three other CENTACs targeted large cocaine organizations from Latin America that operated in the U.S. Yet other CENTACs dismantled criminal groups that manufactured and distributed LSD, PCP and amphetamines. Rob had been assigned to a star unit, CENTAC 16, in 1979. CENTAC 16 was split into West Coast and East Coast investigations, and extended its investigations into Mexico, Puerto Rico, Dominican Republic, along with Central and South America. They had dismantled a major international heroin organization, three import groups, and five major distribution networks. In addition, seized approximately $1 million and reaped another $1 million in bail left by fleeing defendants. CENTAC 16 ultimately indicted 100 major traffickers, along with 61 lesser criminals. The CENTAC program was considered extremely successful. According to a 1980 General Accounting Office Report: "The results of CENTAC investigations have been impressive, not only in terms of the number of high-level traffickers arrested, but also the sentences the traffickers have received. CENTAC results are impressive considering the small percentage of the DEA's enforcement effort CENTAC comprised." Using only three percent of the DEA's enforcement staff and one point three percent of its expenditures for information and evidence, CENTAC arrested 2,116 traffickers. This total represented over twelve percent of all Class I violators arrested by the DEA over a three-year period, including the timeframe of Rob Anderson's involvement. They weren't all his busts, but he had a nice slice of the pie. Problem was, they never seemed to get the Top Dogs. Like the Menolos family in California. They seemed to be untouchable. A very curious thing.

The DEA assigned Rob as an instructor in the Basic Agent training class, which comprised twelve weeks. Students trained from 9 a.m. to 8 p.m. and allowed only five days off, receiving what would be equivalent to sixteen weeks of training. The rigorous schedule insured that DEA agents-in-training would be well-prepared to face the challenges ahead of them. The training class included courses in field training and report writing exercises, as well as the addition of a three-day conspiracy school. Students also spent many hours studying law, in response to the DEA's increasing focus on conspiracy cases and to a survey of agents in the field that showed more training would be helpful. Basic agents received increased training in the use of technical investigative aids and new conspiracy techniques. Rob's classes were quite popular because of his recent and near-legendary experience in the trenches.

Rob was in the groove. His MBA classes began in late March and his classes at the Training Facility were filled with energized trainees. Yep, in the groove… until the call came from Bobby Spragg, on April 26th.

"Rob, you sittin' down?" Bobby's voice was as serious as Rob had ever heard it.

"What's up, big guy?" Rob had a hunch he wouldn't like the answer.

"You ain't gonna believe this shit. We found Harker and James," Spragg hesitated, "both dead, in the back of Cody's pickup truck. But wait, there's more…the fucking truck was impounded by the Davenport police back in February!"

"What the ever-loving fuck!" exclaimed Rob. "You gotta be shitting me!"

"Oh, it gets better. They actually sent notices of impoundment to Cody's freakin' house after they towed it! Then it sat in their impound yard for three months, with the James Gang in the fucking bed, covered with snow and brush! Heads bashed in with a wood splitting wedge or some shit. Then, they sold the truck at auction to two farm boys, who uncovered the bodies. You can't make this shit up, brother."

Rob was stunned. "What happened to our BOLO, man? Are those guys all idiots, or what? Whose shit-show is this?"

"We're still working on all that. Just got the word on this yesterday from the Detectives in Davenport and Iowa State Police. At least somebody was smart enough to add up all the pieces and make a call."

"Suspects?" Rob was not expecting an affirmative answer.

"All things considered, we ain't got shit. They've been laying up in that truck bed since Christmas. Not much left to go with. Other than the natural process of decomposition, the critters have had their go, too. Only saving grace is the cold weather and snow cover. Pretty obvious cause of death, though—their heads were both bashed in. Neither of these guys were wimps, so it's obvious that this was a hit. Execution by crushing of skulls. If I wasn't so well ingrained inside the organization, I'd be looking at the Reapers. Brutality like this is a hallmark of the biker gangs. But, in this case, something this dramatic, I'd have heard something. And none of our sources has heard a damn thing." The frustration in Bobby's voice was palpable.

"You need me back out there?" Rob figured he could get some time allocated for that.

"Nah, not at this time," Spragg replied, "we just have to work the traps. Our theory is pretty straight forward: either the boys did a deal with the wrong buyers, or they stepped on some mighty big toes. Results are what we see here. I'll keep you informed." With that, he hung up the phone.

Rob Anderson wasn't a man who suffered from regrets. His philosophies were more in line with the "Shit Happens, deal with it" school of life. But this one bothered him. More than it should, though he wasn't sure why. Just a couple more drug dealers, unequivocally out of circulation—so what. But there was a 'what.' Rob wasn't sure why, but his gut wouldn't let this one go. He filed the currently known info away in his mental filing system. He had plenty to focus on, now—Bobby would let him know if anything further cropped up.

Chapter 12—Swordfish

Rob kept his focus on the job and his education, but he was hungry for some bigger action. He needed the adrenalin rush of being in the hunt—the thrill of the kill, as they say. He stayed on top of the various operations that the DEA and their partner agencies had underway, hoping to find a way to at least get his toes wet again. Toward the end of 1980, that hope turned into reality. An opportunity to leverage his growing education and his experience in interdiction of drug conspiracies. It also meant that attaining his MBA would need to be put on hold for a while.

In December, the DEA launched a major investigation in Miami aimed at international drug organizations. The operation was dubbed Operation Swordfish because it was intended to snare the "big fish" in the drug trade. The DEA set up a bogus money laundering operation in suburban Miami Lakes that was called "Dean International Investments, Inc." Cute way to incorporate "DEA" into the name. Not as cute as a band named "SPOC," but it was still funny. The DEA installed Rob as the head of the front company, assuming the undercover identity of 'Frank Dean,' president of Dean Investments. To pull off this operation, DEA agents teamed up with a Cuban exile who had fallen on hard times and willing to lure Colombian traffickers to the bogus bank.

Besides spending time in Cuban prisons after the Bay of Pigs invasion, Alejandro David Castillo had also served jail time in the U.S. for tax fraud and was heavily in debt to the U.S. Internal Revenue Service. More recently, they had busted Castillo in a very nice boat with a very nice-looking lady and a very large brick of Bolivian cocaine. He was ready to do whatever the DEA wanted, to avoid a stint at Club Fed. DEA assigned Rob as Castillo's handler, working closely to make sure that the deals came down just as the DEA needed them to. Very familiar territory, for the seasoned DEA Special Agent.

This gig came with some unique challenges, however. The primary target was a cocaine ring led from Colombia by a man named Carlos Jader Alvarez, known as El Muñeco (the doll). El Muñeco's group was notorious for their unique way of dealing with informants. Usually involving chainsaws and shower stalls. The drug lords of the Medellin cartel were not all that particular about who they killed. Cops were always on the menu, along with anyone else who got in their way. Rob did his work in a designer suit—but with his trusted Remington-Rand 1911 always tucked neatly into his armpit.

At the center of the sting set up was a group of DEA undercover operatives, who acted as high-rolling money launderers. They worked from a plush-carpeted Miami office suite with rented Cadillacs parked outside, a well-stocked liquor cabinet, a chest-high safe and a high-speed money-counting machine. Their offices were also equipped, discreetly, with video cameras and tape machines to record what was going on. The sting was multi-agency, however, including FBI, IRS and, while not overt about it, CIA was also involved. CIA was very active in central and south America—all the other agencies knew that they would have the Langley Boys paying attention to everything related to this operation. There were a couple of the FBI guys that were cool, though, in Rob's mind. One, Keven McMenimen, was great. He was continually trying to get Rob to change agencies.

"You know," McMenimen said one day, "DEA stands for 'Drunk Every Afternoon! You need to come over to the serious party!

"Oh, you mean to 'Famous But Incompetent?'" Rob gave it right back, "I think I'll stay over here on the 'dark side,' where the bad guys fear our name!" This banter was the civilian agency equivalent to the razz between every branch of the military. All in fun—but each would have the other's back when the shit came down.

For months, Rob and the other agents did business from the office in a tree-shaded shopping center in the northwest Miami Lakes area, drawing the alleged drug smugglers more deeply into the charade with 'seed money' from the Federal Reserve Bank. The cash went to buy cocaine and fund bank accounts created to give the appearance of large-scale money activity. Of course, the most challenging part of the investigation was luring the first few customers into the fake operation. Agents at first relied on informers inside the drug underworld, led their way by Castillo, but once Dean International Investments Inc. became known within the community of drug smugglers, it generated its own business. That did not make it any safer for Castillo, Rob, or any of the other Agents. One slip and they might all have a "gas explosion" accident. Or worse.

"It takes terrific informants to get people to introduce people to you," Rob was looking at Castillo, but speaking to the Operations Team, "but once they get the first pickle out of the jar, things get easier. These fucks will beat a path to our doorway."

Castillo spoke up, "I'm just trying to do what I can. I'm counting on you people to live up to your end of the deal. I want a nice new house in a nice new town with a nice new identity. And soon. If these Medellin dudes figure me out, I'm gonna be shark bait."

The DEA had a history of throwing informants—sometimes referred to as 'chumps'—directly under the bus. Rob knew this but remained determined to live up to his deal with Castillo. The Cuban had had several opportunities to roll over on the entire operation. He hadn't. He deserved the right outcome. Sadly, it didn't work out that way.

By April 1981, the operation had moved to a bigger and still more luxurious office suite two miles away, adding to the impression of big-time dealing. Things were going quite nicely. During the eighteen-month investigation, Rob and his Operation Swordfish Multi-Agency Team were able to gather enough evidence for a federal grand jury to indict sixty-seven U.S. and Colombian citizens.

The most tough part of any undercover operation was knowing when to stop—whether the risk of blowing the cover was worth whatever additional evidence could be accumulated. With Operation Swordfish, that decision was made for them. One

Saturday night, at a hot South Beach disco, Rob had arranged to buy sixty kilos of coke for which payment was due the following Friday—more than $3 million at the going wholesale rates. This was an enormous deal with a lot of cash trading hands. Rob called the play—they would use this one to wrap-up the operation.

"Okay, this is the one," he told the Operations Chief, in DC, "we need to spring the trap. We have enough to indict a shitload of people. Some of those will plea bargain and probably lead us to even bigger fish," Rob had to get the 'fish,' part in there, "and could make a serious dent in the cartel operations in the States."

With approval from the DEA leadership at the I Street headquarters, the Operation Swordfish Team—DEA Agents, FBI Agents and IRS Agents—kicked off the series of arrests, the Friday that the payment was due on the big buy. It was the culmination of eighteen months of expensive, dangerous work. The climax also included some frustrations for the entire alphabet of agents, however.

First, Attorney General William French Smith announced the indictments and plans to sweep Miami for suspects more than an hour before the sweep had actually begun. Brilliant. As expected, the early disclosure beamed all over Miami instantaneously in newscasts, endangering lives of everyone at 'Dean International Investment, LLC' by giving the Medellin Cartel thugs time to react. Which they did.

Rob got a call at his desk phone at the Dean offices as the morning wore on, asking if he had heard the news of a big drug bust under way. "All good over here, man. I heard the reports, but we are cool."

Soon afterward, the drug smugglers dropped by with eleven kilos and were busted on the spot. That's when thing went to shit. As the agents inside the office locked down the three coke dealers, Rob and Castillo went out the door to Rob's rented Caddie.

"Watch your six!" the shout was from Castillo. His last words.

Rob dropped to the sidewalk just as the automatic MAC-10 opened up, raking the side of the Eldorado Biarritz. He had his 1911 out and in action, even before his knee hit the concrete. Two shooters—until Rob fired. One shooter, still emptying his magazine, directly into Alejandro David Castillo. Two FBI Agents ran out of the office and fired on the second shooter, as did Rob Anderson. The threat was terminated, but so was one of the good guys.

Castillo never had a chance. This guy got the shaft every time he turned around. He had been part of the Bay of Pigs invasion—left to twist in the wind, by the CIA. He had also been a real-estate investor and electronics dealer who had got in trouble with the I.R.S. over some of his real-estate deals. He had served a few months in a minimum-security Federal lockup and ended up hopelessly in debt to the Government. Thing is, in this case, Castillo was the key to the success of Operation Swordfish. He had schmoozed his way into the good graces—and probably the bed—of Marlene Navarro, the Money Queen of the El Muñeco organization.

"Well, amigo, you have fully paid your debt," thought Anderson.

At the conclusion of the operation, the Task Force had seized 100 kilos of cocaine, a quarter-million methaqualone pills—'ludes' was the street name—tons of marijuana, and $80,000,000 in cash, cars, land and Miami bank accounts. Operation Swordfish resulted in a significant attack on South Florida's flourishing drug trade. Par for the course, at least one of the investigation's major targets, Ms. Marlene Navarro, escaped arrest. It seems she had left town about two weeks prior to the bust and had been spotted in Medellin. No one knew whether she got wind of the sting or simply traveled to Colombia on one of her frequent 'business trips' there. Rob did not believe in coincidences.

Still, Navarro was charged in one of the sixty-seven indictments, as being the ring leader of the major cocaine smuggling and money-laundering operation. Thanks to Castillo, she had been duped into laundering more than $6 million in a dozen transactions with the DEA's dummy financial services firm. Truth be told, Rob kinda liked Marlene. She was funny, smart, dressed to kill—and she was absolutely gorgeous. That she had nerves of steel and enjoyed living on the edge only added to the attraction. Ah, the fickleness of fate.

Swordfish also ended the careers of many 'upstanding citizens,' including a local prosecutor, three bank employees, two lawyers and a plastic surgeon—along with more than a few members of the Task Force. Cash is just too seductive for some people—even federal agents. When the final count was in, there was a minor issue related to millions of missing dollars. Closing the books on this gig was probably the most universally agreed decision that the multi-agency world had ever come to. There were a lot of sweaty palms when the General Accounting Office announced their upcoming investigation and audit. Rob saw this one coming, but never lost a minute of sleep. Integrity is the enemy of insomnia.

Chapter 13—Exit Strategy

In January 1983, Rob Anderson returned to Washington, DC to finish his education and to continue to teach at the Training Facility. The next five years, leading up to his retirement, were filled with a heavy workload for the DEA. Cocaine was everywhere. Crack cocaine had come in hard and fast, mostly out of South-Central Los Angeles, controlled by the Crips and the Bloods. In 1985, Rob learned about a strong indication of knowledge of the drug operations, at the highest levels of the political and intelligence establishments. Turns out the boys from Langley had deals going with the Nicaraguan Contra Rebels, who were in turn in bed with the Cartels, and suspected of helping a certain group of Nicaraguan smugglers based in California. Rob also learned that back in February 1982, CIA director William Casey sought—and Attorney General William French Smith approved—a special exemption freeing the agency from legal requirements to report about the drug trafficking operations of its assets. Another 'coincidence' that just 'happened' to develop, just as the DEA was working to take down a Colombian Cartel's business in Miami.

"Ain't that some shit?" Rob thought, when he heard that last bit of news. "Can't help but wonder how long that crap has been going down. We're over here trying to break the chain and hit them in the bank account, and these pukes are helping them game the fucking system! God Bless America," Rob lifted a toast towards Virginia.

For the past three years, Rob had been submitting clarifications and depositions to the mucky-mucks upstairs, along with investigators from GAO. The Miami thing was a real mess. Over $20 million came and went through the operation. Not much of it was left to be found. GAO was doing everything short of using a proctoscope on every member of the multi-agency team. A few had been easy to uncover—hard to buy a new Mercedes or Lincoln on Federal wages. These were the small fish. Everyone knew there were bigger ones to fry.

"Anderson? McMenimen here," the call came in on Rob's newly issued cellular telephone, "I'd like to catch up with you. Off the record. Got time for a drink?"

Rob liked Kevin. A straight shooter. Came from a family of Feds. "Sure, man. How about dinner, too? Filamena's?" Great Italian sounded like just the ticket, and Filamena was top of the mark. "I'll make the reservation for 1900."

"Oh, hell yes," Came the reply, "I love the way you think! See you there."

Filomena had been serving up an unparalleled Italian fine-dining experience in Georgetown since 1983. It is heralded for its traditional cuisine, fine wine and exceptional service. Rob went there as often as he could afford to go.

"How's business?" The FBI Agent was grinning, "I hear you boys ain't got shit to do!"

"Let's review," countered the DEA Agent, "cocaine on every corner; crack houses in every inner-city from Los Angeles to Portland, Maine, DEA Agents being kidnapped and murdered… nah… we're working half days. Any twelve hours we choose!"

"Shit man, sorry," Kevin's expression showed his sincerity, "I just heard about your guy in Guadalajara. That's fucked up, brother."

"Sure is. Kiki Camerena was one of the good guys. A patriot and a man of honor. I worked with Kiki on the Ft. Ord bust, back in 1978. He was a Marine, before joining us. Did a tour in the Nam about the same time as me, but up north in I

Corps. Nobody deserves to go out like he did. Fucking savages."

"I heard the story, man, kidnapped and tortured. Bad deal." Kevin lowered his gaze.

"Well, *c'est la guerre*, as they say. The best part is, he took down the biggest pot operation in the Baja, before they got to him! To Kiki!" Both men raised their glasses. "What's on your mind, big guy?" Rob asked.

"How many years you got, before your twenty? Can't be many, right? Given any thought to your next move?" The FBI Agent clearly had something up his sleeve.

"I've got right at three left," Rob was smiling, "figured I'd do some fishing, then maybe give the private sector a go. I gotta say, I'm damn well frustrated by the internal BS we're dealing with right now. I can't prove anything, but it sure seems like the boys over in Langley are doing their best to block us from popping some of the biggest traffickers in the business. I'm getting fed up with this shit!"

"I'm with you, brother," came the reply, "and you aren't wrong. We see it, too. It's all about our support of the Contras, down in Nicaragua. That was testified to in a drug trial, last year. You remember the 'Frogman Case,' right? Some sketchy shit, that's for sure. Which leads me to my point of asking you to join me tonight. I'm retiring next year. Myself and a couple of others are planning to start a consulting firm, focused on the retail industry. Helping them to reduce what they call 'shrink'—large scale theft from warehouses and the supply chain. We're doing some of that work now, in the Bureau, but there's so much more that can be done. Big bucks to be made, too. We think you would be a great fit for the new firm. Interested?"

Rob found the concept intriguing but wanted to give it some more thought. He told Kevin that and they dove into the amazing fare and the even more amazing wine. Rob promised Kevin an answer within the next few days, and the men went their own way.

It was a restless night. Rob couldn't stop thinking about that whole business with the Menolos crew out west. "What's up with this guy?" he thought. Susan Smith, a top-shelf DEA operator, had opened up an investigation on Menolos, back in 1981. Smith had picked up rumors on the street that a group of Nicaraguan exiles headed by Menolos was selling cocaine in the Bay Area and sending money and weapons back to Central America. She checked the DEA files on Menolos and found a bulging record of the man's criminal activities, dating back to a 1978 FBI report charging that he and his brother Ernesto were 'smuggling 20 kilos of cocaine at a time into the United States.'

One of the entry points for Norwin **Menolos**' cocaine was apparently New Orleans, where Smith came across records from the DEA's 'Operation Alligator.' This government sting had busted a large cocaine ring in New Orleans. One of the arrested men told a DEA Special Agent that Menolos was the source of the cocaine. However, Menolos was never arrested. To add insult to injury, a couple of years ago, in February 1983, the FBI had scored one of the largest cocaine seizures in California history, in the so-called Frogman Case. They had caught members of the Menolos drug syndicate attempting to swim ashore at the San Francisco docks from a Colombian freighter, with 400 pounds of cocaine. According to the DEA, the drugs had a street value of more than $100 million. Ultimately, thirty-five people were arrested in the Frogman case, including a Menolos henchman, whose house Susan Smith had staked out, known as Carlos Cabezas. The Frogman trial was going on at the very moment the DEA was telling Susan Smith that information about Cabezas and Menolos held no interest.

The Frogman Case was not exactly your run-of-the-mill drug trial. On November 28, 1984, Cabezas testified in that trial that this cocaine-smuggling operation was a funding source for the Contras.

He testified that the cocaine he brought into the US came from Norwin Menolos' ranch in Costa Rica, and that the CIA was aware of the operation. His testimony at the trial was limited because the judge would not allow the defense to explore the CIA's role in any detail. Menolos was not indicted. Yep, sketchy shit, for sure. This was not what Rob had signed up for.

Time to line up the exit strategy.

Chapter 14—As Time Goes By

Over the next three years, Rob continued to train new Agents at the Facility, while completing his MBA at Georgetown. He also kept his hand in the game by worming his way in to some interesting DEA operations. There was plenty to go around, with the insane increase in cocaine smuggling into America. In 1985, one of the more interesting operations was 'Operation Rough Rider'—a three-year joint undercover operation by the FBI, DEA and various state police agencies. That operation resulted in arrests of over 100 members of the Hells Angels motorcycle gang on **charges of running a coast-to-coast narcotics ring**. The operation began three years ago in Baltimore when two FBI agents went undercover with the help of a 'biker' working as a confidential informant.

Agents bought drugs from Hells Angels members from eleven chapters in seven states, an affidavit said, and learned that a percentage of each chapter's drug profits was deposited in the Hells Angels national treasury.

Undercover agents bought $2 million in methamphetamines, cocaine, marijuana, hashish, PCP and LSD from the Hells Angels during the undercover operation. The arrests were made in New York City, Albany, N.Y., New Haven, Conn., Newark,

N.J., the Boston area, Cleveland, Omaha, Neb., Charlotte, N.C., Richmond, Va., New Orleans, Phoenix, San Francisco and Sacramento, Calif.

A major player in the operation was none other than Agent Bobby Spragg, on loan to the joint task force from the Illinois Bureau of Investigation. Rob decided to give the man a call, to bust his chops a bit.

"Bobby freakin Spragg," Rob mustered as much condescending tone as he could, without laughing, "I thought you were Grim Reaper to the bone! Not smelly enough for you?"

"Ha! Fuck you, Snake Eater!" Bobby couldn't hold the laughter. "I'm seemingly the only guy you pukes know, who can speak Biker! How ya been?"

"Livin' the dream, brother, livin' the dream." Got my eyes on the prize—I'm just a few years shy of twenty, then I'm out of this shit. Got a plan to go private sector."

"I feel you, man. The times they are a changin'," Bobby sighed, "and not for the better, much of the time. We have to celebrate every small victory!"

"Well, bro, this one wasn't small," Rob was grinning, "$2 million is a nice haul! But what are you guessing as the source? Any action upstream?"

"We're getting nothing from the Angels, man. Tight lipped, unlike some of the usual street dealers we pop. That said, we're pretty sure it's coming from the Cali Cartel, via a group of Nicaraguans in the US."

"We need to talk, offline," Rob said, "it's a pretty small set of probable players, from my viewpoint. As long as I have you, any developments on the James Gang case? That one still bugs the shit out of me."

"Man," Bobby sounded exasperated, "I wish there was. Local guys and Staties have pretty much filed that one away. Too many current issues to deal with and they've beaten every bush they could find. From my perspective, the silence around the murders makes more noise than a freakin mortar attack. If anyone knows anything—and you can bet that they do—they are either involved or are too scared shitless to speak up. I'm like you, man, I hate loose ends."

The two men made plans to catch up later about Rob's speculations around the source of the Hells Angels' drug supply. Everything seemed to point to the same people. No one could say for certain if the Menolos organization was involved, but, as the old joke goes, 'if the foo shits, wear it...'

When 1988 rolled around, Rob was ready for the Gold Watch. The past six years had been filled with frustrations and an ever-increasing distrust for the cabal of the Departments of State and Justice, along with the Central Intelligence Agency. Sadly, he was also convinced that the Drug Enforcement Administration had been complicit in more than a few cases. Much of that was underscored, beginning in 1986. The Riverside, California office of the FBI initiated a case which included Norwin Menolos and some of his associates. Menolos began cooperating with DEA contacts in Costa Rica, where he had taken up residence. That resulted in outing a couple of his California-based dealers, including Danilo Blandon. Massive amounts of evidence, but amazingly, no arrests. Even after the Organized Crime Drug Enforcement Task Force finally opened a formal case on Blandon, in 1987, San Francisco U.S. Attorney's Office and San Francisco FBI agreed to defer prosecution of Menolos for drug trafficking, pending the outcome of the Los Angeles OCDETF investigation of the Blandon organization. The indictment was sealed.

Something was definitely rotten in Denmark... and in Washington, DC.

By the time he actually separated from the DEA, Rob was already having his paperwork processed with Kevin McMenimen's company, RetailEye, Inc. Their primary focus was on detection and investigation of Organized Retail Crime rings that were having a serious impact on companies, coast to coast. Good work, which allowed Rob to take advantage of not only his investigative background, but his MBA in Forensic Accounting. Their clients were some of the largest retailers in the country and they were making a serious dent in the area of loss prevention. It was a great company. They grew by leaps and bounds and Rob's piece of the action ensured him a very comfortable 'second retirement,' which he took advantage of, sixteen years later. He had planned to go longer, but then, in 2004, he got the call from Bobby Spragg.

Chapter 15—Cold Case

"I hope you're sitting down," were the first words Bobby Spragg spoke into the cell phone, "this is going to rock your world!"

Bobby explained that as the twenty-fifth anniversary of Cody James and Gary Harker's death approached, a friend of theirs — one who'd been entrusted with a certain roll of film — opened up his nightstand. He pulled out the photos he'd had printed twenty-five years earlier. Apparently, he figured the time had come, and he knew what he had to do. He contacted the Davenport, Iowa police, who, in turn, contacted the DEA and the Illinois Bureau of Investigations. Friends inside the Bureau contacted Bobby, himself long retired. Davenport police announced they were renewing the investigation into the double homicide.

"This fucking guy turned over twenty-five-year-old photos of suspects they believe to be involved in the killing," Bobby said, "I knew you'd want to know."

"Jesus H Christ!" Rob was incredulous. "You just can't make this shit up! Have you seen the pictures?"

"Not yet," came the reply, "but I'm working on getting them. My pals at the Bureau will come through, I'm sure of that. Just playing the waiting game. The investigating detective from Davenport says he has reason to believe that the photos were taken in Bolinas, California—a coastal village about thirty miles north of San Francisco. They've sent copies out to the Marin County cops, to see if they can ID the two guys in the pictures."

"Bolinas. I know it well. When I was working the Ft. Ord case, we suspected that shit was coming in through that area, then trickling down to Frisco and points south. Trickle may be too weak a term—more like a torrent. To make matters more interesting, we suspected that members of the Menolos organization had at least one place up that way. Nicaraguans," Rob paused, "remember what the dude at the auto shop said about the guy who picked up the compressor? 'A Latin accent, but not Mexican'—things are falling into place in my head, and I don't like the shapes they're forming. Please keep me tuned in—and try to get me a copy of the pictures."

Rob had been following the case of Norwin Menolos, his family and their organization, since 1980. Here was a guy known as the "Nicaraguan Mafia," clear ties to everything from murder, drug and weapons smuggling, auto theft and assassinations to counterfeiting, yet cases and charges against him simply dissolved. Massive amounts of cocaine could be attributed to his cartel. He claimed to be involved with the CIA and their efforts to finance the Contras. Now, Rob had the strong cop-hunch that someone in the Menolos food chain might be involved in two murders halfway across the country from his comfortable California Kingdom.

In August 1996, finally shedding the light of day on things Rob Anderson already knew or suspected, the San Jose Mercury News had published the 'Dark Alliance,' series of articles alleging that cocaine was 'virtually unobtainable in black neighborhoods before members of the CIA's army'—the Nicaraguan Contras—started bringing it into South-Central Los Angeles in the 1980s. The articles stated that Danilo Blandon, identified as a former Contra leader and a supplier of cocaine to Los Angeles drug dealer Ricky Ross, had testified in court that his cocaine profits supported the Contras, and that Blandon's attorney had concluded that Blandon was selling cocaine for the CIA.

The articles also reported that major narcotics trafficker known as Norwin Menolos had a relationship with the Contras, that CIA or others had hampered the criminal investigation of

Menolos and that a relative alleged Norwin had financed the Contras.

Further, the articles claimed that Carlos Cabezas, who had been convicted in a 1983 San Francisco drug prosecution known as 'The Frogman Case,' was connected to Menolos and that Cabezas had obtained cocaine from a drug trafficker who had contact with the Contras. Finally, the articles reported that funds that had been seized from a leader of the prosecuted drug ring had been returned to him by the U.S. Attorney's Office because of his claim that the money belonged to the Contras.

As expected, the Central Intelligence Agency had issued a vehement denial of any involvement between themselves and smuggling drugs to help fund the Contras. In 1998, the CIA published their "findings:"

"No information has been found to indicate that any past or present employee of CIA, or anyone acting on behalf of CIA, had any direct or indirect dealing with the individual known as Norwin Menolos or Danilo Blandon. Additionally, no information has been found to show that any of these individuals was ever employed by CIA, or met by CIA employees or anyone acting on CIA's behalf."

The report concluded that Menolos had no CIA connection and made only modest contributions to the Contras. The failure to prosecute him was a result not of federal intervention on his behalf but of long-standing problems in federal anti-drug efforts.

"In short, the investigation of Menolos failed because of inadequate resources devoted to this case and inadequate coordination between law enforcement agencies, which are recurring law enforcement issues," the study said.

What a surprise.

Volume II of the 1998 OIG Report told a different story. The CIA was not only aware of the drug smuggling activities, but they were also installing drug kingpins as leaders of the Contras! Sadly, by the time Rob learned about the uncovered pictures, it was too late for the first guy to cry out about this debacle. The mainstream press had ridiculed Gary Webb, the author of the "Dark Alliance" expose. He had been ostracized by his peers, and forced to leave his job. More, he could never get another job as a journalist. In his resulting despair, Gary took his own life, just two weeks before Rob got the call from Bobby Spragg. Even that act was highly suspicious, as Gary's 'suicide' death had resulted from two gunshots to his head.

Seems Mr. Webb had taken on the wrong people in his fight for truth.

It was Rob Anderson's experience that smoke was usually the result of fire. While he knew that the various federal law enforcement and investigative agencies were, at times, bumbling idiots, in his twenty years of service he had never seen that occur on this grand a level. Far too many "coincidences" here. Rob did not believe in coincidences. One screw up—sure. Two or more, on the same case—possible, but unlikely. Continual screw ups on such a massive scale—NFW. Not without some back-office puppeteering. That, thought the old pro, was a problem.

With the unique opportunity to move into a now well-funded second retirement, Rob Anderson decided that he was going to do some independent investigation—he was bound and determined to get to the bottom of the cold case of Gary Harker and Cody James' murder. For Rob, it had been nothing 'cold.' It was always simmering in the back of his mind. What had he missed, 25 years ago? It was time to clear things up if he could.

Chapter 16—Chasing Ghosts

Through the first half of 2005, Rob Anderson split his time between helping Kevin prepare for his imminent departure and researching all he could about the Menolos organization, Iran-Contra, the CIA and their relationships with his own alma mater, the Drug Enforcement Administration. Research was so much easier these days—the internet had changed everything. That was the good news and the bad news. Rob was often exasperated, frequently shocked—but never truly surprised at what he was uncovering.

It would have been great if I'd had the chance to speak with Gary Webb, Rob thought. The guy was a walking encyclopedia about this operation.

Obviously, that wouldn't happen, so Rob had to rely on the details he could gather from the various websites and databases, plus calling in a few favors for 'chats' with some of his old DEA cronies. Kevin McMenimen was also helpful by reaching out to his old pals in the Bureau. Neither entity was all that cozy with the folks from Langley. Too many of their cases had taken unusual turns—they often lay the suspicion right on the front steps of The Company. In the good news department, though,

Rob got lots of names and pointers to folks that had been involved in the dealings of the 1980s—on both sides of the law.

The pictures that Bobby Spragg sent him in February were also quite helpful. Again, good news and bad news. The Marin County Sheriff's Office could identify one of the people, after they passed the photos around among retired law enforcement personnel. A Nicaraguan named Rudolfo Sanchez Flores. He was well-known to them for a couple of reasons. One, he was on their hit parade for a major takedown, back in 1980. They believed him to be a top dog in a cocaine smuggling operation, using boats brought into the docks in Bolinas. He had a leased estate there, right on the ocean. Two, they found him in four pieces on that same estate, a week before he was to be arrested. There were no viable suspects in the murder. They also suspected Flores of being affiliated with the Menolos Organization. They also published the photos in a Marin County newspaper, including their internet edition, hoping locals would recognize some of the other men. So far, no one had come forward.

"Spragg," Rob was constantly amazed in the technology involved with cell phones, "I hope I'm keeping you from something good, like baiting another catfish hook!" Bobby had sworn the after he retired, fishing for catfish would be the most strenuous part of his day.

"Ha!" Bobby always had been ready with a laugh, "this is what retirement is supposed to be like. Not like you, you fucking workaholic! What's on your mind?"

"Well, sir, I'm planning a bit of an adventure, starting in beautiful downtown Davenport, Iowa. I figured I'd invite you along for as much of the ride as your fat, lazy ass can handle. What say you?"

"I was wondering when you'd get around to this. I'm surely in for the first part. Hell, it's my back yard. I'll let you know about anything further, once we see what that may be," said Spragg, "When are you coming this way?"

"I just got off a call with the investigating detective from Davenport PD, Greg Keller. Seems like a solid guy. I have an appointment to meet with him, next Friday," there was more than a tinge of energy in Rob's voice, "he was excited to connect with us, considering our history with the James Gang. I'll be flying in to QCA next Wednesday. Pick me up?"

"You bet, amigo! See you then—we have some beers that need drinking and lies that need telling!" Spragg signed off with a laugh, "it'll be good seeing you, old pal!"

The flight to Quad Cities International Airport was the best kind—uneventful. Rob was amused by the nomenclature "International." He knew that any airport authority could name an airport 'international,' if they chose to, but the biggest criteria, in Rob's experience, would include actually having Customs facilities or some infrastructure to support flights from other countries. Not likely to have a DC10 from Singapore landing out here in the middle of the USA.

Bobby Spragg was waiting for Rob near the baggage claim. After a handshake and a couple of solid shoulder slaps, they walked to the parking lot to jump into Bobby's Ford F-150 pickup truck.

"A pickup," Rob tried to sound as sarcastic as he could, "why am I not surprised. Once a shitkicker, always a shitkicker!"

"Well, I considered bringing the Harley," Bobby laughed, "but I didn't think you'd want to ride bitch!" Both men had a good bellow over that one.

It's good that the meeting is not until tomorrow, Rob thought, the next morning. He and Bobby had hit a few of the local bars, chasing Cuervo with a locally brewed IPA. Thursday morning was rough. The night, however, had been great. There were good stories and old memories, most of which brought on fits of laughter. Rob learned that most of the Reapers that Bobby had invested so many years infiltrating had been busted. He stayed tight with the club for a decade and had infiltrated a couple of other 'prospects' into the mix, who had been positioned to pick up the ball when Bobby retired. His work culminated in 'Operation Iron Horse,' an investigation that uncovered that the bikers had trafficked over 200 pounds of cocaine (worth at least $3 million) over a ten-year period. Finally, in 1999, charges were brought up against eighteen Grim Reapers, including the club's national president. They all went down hard because of solid police work. Bobby also shared that Rob's favorite punk, Rocky, had actually turned over a new leaf. He did eight years in the Indiana State Penitentiary, where he says he was 'born again.' When he got out, he became an ordained minister, with a small church in Southern Illinois. Miracles, apparently, do happen. Unfortunately, the news about old friends and foes was not all good. Agent Peggy Beck had committed suicide in 1985. Her folks found her in her garage, with her 12-gauge at her feet. This was sad news. Rob had really liked Agent Peggy. Sadly, she wasn't the first law enforcement officer he'd known who took that one-way route. Probably wouldn't be the last. Thing was, Peggy never seemed the type, nor had she shown any of the telltale signs of being depressed and suicidal.

Rob ordered three shots of Cuervo. "To Peggy," he toasted, knocking back one shot and pouring one on the floor of the bar.

"To Peggy Beck!" Spragg finished his shot and slammed the glass on the bar. "Now, I've got to get my ass to bed!"

The Davenport detective met the two retired cops with a smile, a handshake and an offer of not-terrible coffee. The Meeting was in one of the conference rooms at the cop shop, on Harrison Street, a few blocks up from the Mississippi River. It could have been any other police station in any other town. The vibe was always the same.

"Welcome back to the party, gentlemen," said the detective, "I'm hoping we can help one another to close this case. Based on my outreach over the past couple of months, though, my expectations are not high," he said that when he'd first opened the file — the first time the case had been reviewed since 1996 — he found, "there were things that weren't done that needed to be done and should have been done."

Keller explained that many of the people the victims hung around with were also involved in drugs and would not go to the police in 1979-80, but twenty-five years later were more willing to answer investigators' questions and provide evidence. The ones talking now, he said, were the same ones who listened to James and Harker talk about concerns for their safety a quarter-century ago.

"People talking to us now are speaking freely and not fearing retaliation," Keller said. "Now that we have better investigative tools in our arsenal, we're hoping for more definitive data. The soil and shrubbery found in the truck was tested to determine whether it matched similar materials from a suspected murder site, though we would not disclose the location to anyone we want to question—you know the drill—we believe the site was an old truck stop out on Highway 22."

He went on to say that he remained optimistic about the direction of the renewed investigation. It already had turned up hair and blood samples on old evidence for possible DNA analysis—a toolset that wasn't available in 1980. In fact, an evidence technician used a chemical process just being developed at the time of the slayings to find a fingerprint on evidence discovered in the truck with the bodies.

"Any hits on the prints?" Rob knew that if the person who left it wasn't in any criminal, military or other databases, it wouldn't mean a thing.

"Not at this time," it was the reply both Rob and Bobby expected, "what we do know is, it doesn't match either Harker or

James, nor anyone in our local, regional or Fed databases. A ghost."

"What about the DNA?" Bobby was sure he already knew that answer, too.

"Same shit. Harker and James, of course, and the two clodhoppers from Muscatine who bought the truck, but nothing else."

Davenport Police Department had little more in 2004 than in 1980. Except the pictures. Those pictures were the only solid leads… and they were about as solid as jungle mist in the A Shau Valley. But they were a starting point. Next stop for Rob would be the DEA offices in San Francisco, followed by the Marin County Sheriff's Office. Rob and Bobby extended their thanks to Detective Keller, with promises to mutually share anything they turned up.

"Up for a road trip, Marine?" Bobby would be a good teammate to have on this one.

"Well, brother, I'm afraid I'll have to pass. The Ex is going through some health problems right now. I guess I'll never quite be over her—can't leave her without someone to run her errands and stuff. If you get in a bind though, pop smoke—you know I'll cover your ass!"

Rob was disappointed, but it was cool. Bobby had filled him in on losing the love of his life to the job. Cops suck in relationships, more often than not. Had to respect the loyalty—and he knew Bobby wasn't blowing smoke about being there if Rob needed him. Anderson made a few calls to his pals in DEA HQ, which now shared some high-class space with the FBI, out at Quantico. Seemed like a good marriage, he thought. Many of the folks now seated in Executive Row were once newbies who trained under Rob. He had no problem in getting connected with the 'New Guard' at the DEA San Francisco Branch. He also got contact info for some of the former agents that had been around during the 80s with some involvement in the Menolos Organization investigations.

Rob booked his flights and reserved his rental car at SFO. Time to chase some ghosts!

Chapter 17—West Coast Turnaround

Rob opted to drive his rental to Chicago for a non-stop flight to SFO—San Francisco International. His philosophy about flying was simple: Takeoffs are optional; Landings are mandatory. He wasn't afraid to fly, in fact, he loved flying. He just hated the takeoff and landing parts. That's when most of the bad things happen. He knew that research had shown that takeoff and landing are statistically more dangerous than any other part of a flight. Forty-nine percent of all fatal accidents happen during the final descent and landing phases of the average flight, while fourteen percent of all fatal accidents happen during takeoff and initial climb out. No sense pressing my odds, Rob thought. Besides, he enjoyed driving. Plenty of time to think. And he had plenty to think about.

The six-hour flight from O'Hare to SFO was comfortable. Rob hadn't flown coach since leaving the DEA. His American Airlines flight was equipped with in-flight internet service, so he fired up his laptop. It still amazed him, the advances in technology over the course of the past decade. He harbored a conspiracy-theory idea that it was due to captured alien spaceships out in Area 51. Whatever, he was also thankful that it wasn't a thing during his active undercover years. No way would he have been able to pull off the ruses and deceptions he'd managed to get by with if all this had been available! He felt bad for today's cops—and figured it would only get worse.

The first email Rob sent was to one of his proteges, Joseph Ringheisen, who now had the corner office in the DEA San Francisco Headquarters location on Golden Gate Avenue. As Regional Director, JR knew Rob was coming, but it wouldn't hurt to start the ball rolling. Rob asked to have access to any files on one Rudolfo Sanchez Flores. He also wanted to reach out to Susan Smith, who had done the most extensive research on Menolos, back in the day. He was hoping she might offer some help on Flores and the other guys in the twenty-five-year-old snapshots. After a few minutes, the reply came back. Since Rob and Kevin were still doing certain contract work for the FBI and DEA, his current security clearances would allow him review some of the available information, but maybe not all of it—much of the data was heavily redacted. As for Susan, JR wrote he would see what he could arrange. After a couple of more unsuccessful Yahoo searches for anything he could find about Flores, Rob's laptop battery was shot. He signed off and caught some sleep while he could. Ranger Doctrine dictates: Sleep when you can; Eat when you can. Never know when the next opportunity will be!

As he drifted off, Rob couldn't help wondering whether in-flight internet was available on the planes used in the 9/11 Terror Attacks. He hoped it had been and that some passengers had sent one last 'I love you' email to their families. Crazy how the mind will wander, he thought. It was still too fresh in his mind, that terrible day. He thought about it every time he boarded a plane. He and Kevin had been in Manhattan that crushing day, presenting a proposal to Macy's. They were fortunate to have hotel rooms, which they invited some of the Macy's team to share—no one was leaving the island that day. Rob and Kevin felt the same as most of America's veterans and law enforcement officers—if they hadn't been past the acceptable age, both men would have re-enlisted that very day.

He awoke with almost three hours of flight time remaining. Quite a change, from the first couple of years following 9/11/2001. In those years, Rob would never sleep on a plane. He always booked an aisle set in the last row of First Class, and he always informed the flight crew of his background, on boarding. Every American was apprehensive. Rob Anderson was prepared.

After a trip to the lav, He settled in for the remainder of the ride. Checking the available in-flight movie list, Rob had to laugh when he saw the listing for the 2001 movie, 'Swordfish.' He loved Travolta movies, and this was a pretty good one. And nothing too terrible about Halle Barry, he thought. What was funny was the premise. They loosely based it on his own Operation Swordfish, from 1981 to 82. Loosely, because the time frame they describe and the amount of 'slush fund' money was more than a bit off. The operation had officially ended at the end of 1982, not 1986—although the trials and other 'clean-up' work continued through 1987. Further, as far as Rob knew, there was no place near $400 million left in a 'slush fund,' and if there had been, inflating that to $9.5 billion would have meant an interest rate of over twenty-one percent—more than double the highest rates available. Nice, if you could get it, Rob thought.

Still, seeing the old flick stirred up other, more relevant thoughts. During the Swordfish sting, the CI Castillo was told by Ms. Navarro about a Colombian who was dealing with traffickers in California. Navarro told him that a guy named Ricardo Jatter was responsible for distributing cocaine in California for the Medellin Cartel. That information also came out in a U.S. Court of Appeals trial in 1989, in which they had called Rob to testify. As far as Rob was aware, the Menolos Organization was getting their coke from the Medellin Cartel—

who have no love lost for the guys from Cali. He had to wonder how deep this rabbit hole was going to go…

After landing at SFO and getting his Avis rental car, Rob called his old friend JR, "Landed, amigo. Heading your way now!"

"Best we meet off site," JR seemed cooler than usual, Rob thought, "we need to establish the ground rules. There's a diner just down the block. Can't miss it. I'll get us a table."

"It's your party, buddy," Rob was perturbed, but not angry, "we play by your rules."

The two old pals met in a diner that looked like every other diner Rob had ever been in. A counter, tables and hustling wait staff. JR had a booth near the window, which was cool with Rob. It was always good to see who might come in.

"What's with the cloak and dagger, buddy?" Rob asked, "I'm asking questions about stuff twenty-five years old—I have skivvies older than that."

JR smiled at that but didn't laugh. "I looked into the name you sent and the photos. There's a lot of black in this guy's file. Redacted shit. And not by the DEA. You might want to be careful what you wish for."

"Yeah," Rob sipped his black coffee, "I had a feeling. Still, all I need is a thread. Something that might help me get some closure, not only for my 'one that got away' thing, but both scumbags that were murdered left families. They might want to at least understand the whole story. Call me sentimental."

"So, here's the deal," the DEA Boss began, "in the pictures, we can ID three of the five people. The dominant player you asked about, Rudolfo Sanchez Flores, we know. Marin County told the investigator from Iowa that Flores was Nicaraguan—he wasn't. He was Colombian. He was a member of the Medellin Cartel. We know this, because about a month before he was murdered, in 1980, we busted him with a boat load of coke. He had agreed to become a snitch for the DEA. Two of the other guys were lead dogs in the Menolos organization, out of San Francisco. There's a gringo sitting next to Flores that we can't get a name on, but one of the former Menolos asshats that we later flipped told us he was 'a serious dude, in from New Orleans' to meet with Flores. He also remembers the guy fuming about the 'two punks with a camera, acting like fucking *touristas*.' which is what none of us can figure out—how did two pukes from Hicksville manage to get pictures of these guys and still get home to whichever flyover state they came in from, with all their body parts intact?"

"Medellin?" Rob's curiosity was definitely peaked. "I thought Menolos was getting his coke from the Cali boys. I know from Swordfish that El Muñeco's operators were involved out here, but I assumed they had a different distribution channel. This sounds like grounds for a serious turf war."

"Yessir. You retired in '88, right? That's when The Cali-Medellin war really went into high gear. The serious shit occurred between 1988 and 1993 when the Cali Cartel, under Helmer Herrera and the Medellin Cartel under Pablo Escobar feuded over the rights to drug trafficking in California and the entire United States. The two cartels engaged in a series of assassinations and massacres. They tried to settle things in '93 but couldn't come to terms. It got pretty messy. That's about the time the Menolos boys flipped to the Cali side of things."

"I was tracking a lot of that," Rob said, "glad I was on the fringes. We lost some good folks to that crap. I read about the 'Colombian Folk Art' that the *sicarios* liked to leave behind. Bodies displayed in all kinds of gruesome ways."

"Like Flores, up in Bolinas, JR added.

"Exactly," Rob continued, "I can see how my two dead guys may have been caught up in the mix, but there was no attempt to send a message with their murders. Just the opposite. If they were killed over the flavor of coke they were dealing, it must have been prior to the 'Hollywood' aspects of the deal. What about Susan Smith? Can she add anything?"

"She's graciously declined to chat with you," JR replied, "she said she told all she is willing to tell. She told her ultimate story to the CIA Office of the Inspector General, years ago. Said you can read his report. She confirmed what we already know, and that's what I just told you. I'll leave you with this—though I probably shouldn't—the 'New Orleans dude' in the photos? I asked one of my pals—retired CIA—about the pictures. He seemed to stiffen up a bit when he saw that guy's face. He denied any knowledge, but I think he was bullshitting me. You remember Operation Alligator, back in 1979? And the 'Ollie North Airforce' flights in the Iran-Contra deal, in and out of New Orleans? Our boy Menolos was 'reportedly' all over that fiasco," JR said 'reportedly' with a roll of his eyes and finger-quotes, "along with the cocaine in the return flights from Panama and El Salvador, they were bringing in coke hidden in boat loads of hollowed out lumber," JR finished his cheeseburger, then continued, "look back to '83. We popped that dude in Florida for the same M.O.—coke in a lumber shipment. Turned out that he also owned a warehouse in New Orleans. I'd go out on a limb here, and say where there's wood, there may be fire. It ain't much, but it's the best we can give you."

"Brother, I appreciate everything you've shared, but you could have told me all this in a phone call," Rob was clearly not satisfied, "and saved me a bunch of frequent flyer points, too. Throw me a bone, here. Is your former Menolos CI still on the West Coast? Can you get me a meeting with him?"

"First question first," JR locked eyes with his former colleague, "with as much redaction as these files have, there is no fucking way that I'm talking about it over a phone, of any type. I still feel like I need to check under my car, just because I pulled them up. Next, you know how that shit goes—but I will reach out to him. He's not in California, though, he's outside of Dallas. Hang around for a day or three. Enjoy what's left of our fair city. Try not to trip over one of our 3,000 street people."

With a couple of days to kill, Rob took a drive up the coast to visit Bolinas. He'd already asked Detective Keller from Davenport, to set up a meeting with the Marin County Sheriff. Considering what they had already told Davenport PD, and the time elapsed since 1980, when Flores was murdered, he didn't have high hopes of learning anything new. Hey, what the hell, Rob thought, might as well take a gander at the actual location. He was right about the Marin cops—nothing new to report. Considering that they didn't even know that Flores was Colombian, that wasn't too surprising. The Sheriff himself met with Rob, though, and was good enough to connect him with the investigating officer of the murder case, long since retired.

Former Captain Bill Angelo was happy to join Rob for a beer at Smiley's Schooner Saloon and Hotel, established in 1851 and continually operating ever since. Rob had booked a room there, so it was quite convenient. Smiley's was reported to be the oldest continually operating saloon west of the Mississippi, Rob thought that was cool.

"Pleasure to meet one of the Old Guard." Captain Angelo extended his hand along with a warm smile, "we ancient hunting dogs need to stick together! How can I be of service?"

Rob filled the retired cop in on what he was up to, leaving out a few key details. Never trust a smiling cop, Rob thought. Too many loose ends to fully open the kimono.

"I remember the case, of course," the Captain said, "won't be forgetting that scene for as long as I'm alive. We local boys had been tracking the Flores fellow for a few months. His place was up the cove, with a couple of nice boat slips on the property. He had a good deal of different water-borne visitors in very nice, very fast boats. Pretty clear that something was going on besides fishing." We reported the activity to the DEA folks in Frisco but got the cold shoulder. In fact, we were told to stand the fuck down. We did, but still kept our eyes open whenever Flores was around town. One Sunday—I remember it was Sunday because the Ex and I had just left church—I got the call from our dispatcher. Since my job was Robbery / Homicide, that wasn't a normal thing. Seems Flores' housekeeper had called in, scared shitless. She was too upset to describe the scene, except that it was bad. I dropped the wife off and headed up that way."

"From what I read in the reports, sounds like a damned unpleasant scene," Rob knew that was an understatement.

"Oh yeah," the former detective clearly had a vivid memory of this one, "fucking blood everywhere. We found Flores—what they left of Flores—in the master bathroom. His head and torso were hanging from the showerhead. His legs and arms were in the bathtub. They were removed in sections, apparently, by a chainsaw. We determined they must have started at the knees and elbows, so that Flores could suffer more. They ended the party by giving what was left of him a Colombian Necktie. It was bad," the old cop knocked back a shot of Jack, swishing it in his mouth as if to wash out the taste of those last words, "but we sure got the attention of the Feds—this place was crawling with black SUVs, for weeks!"

"Damn," was all Rob could muster.

"Exactly," spoke Angelo, "I'd take you up to the place, but it's now owned by some rich fucker from Silicon Valley. I guess the history didn't affect the demand, for a place like that one."

The two men finished their evening together with one last toast:

"To retirement!"

The next morning, Rob headed back down the coast to San Francisco. It was a beautiful day, befitting of a ride through this beautiful part of the world. Rob's cell phone rang.

"JR," Rob answered, "what ya got for me?"

"You're all set to meet with the guy now known as Eder Holguin. He lives in a town north of Dallas, called Sherman. That's his new name. Let's leave his former name to the history books, okay? I'll email you with his contact information. He was hesitant, but came around when I told him what you're up to."

Rob extended his thanks, then pressed the end button on his phone. He then called American Airlines reservations for the next flight to Dallas. Being still early, he was able to get out on a 2:00PM non-stop flight that landed in Dallas at 7:40PM Central Time. He called his former secretary at RetailEye to cajole her into setting up a rental car and a hotel. He also asked her to keep Kevin informed of his itinerary.

So went Rob's West Coast turnaround… or maybe it was a runaround?

Chapter 18—A Pillar of the Community

The four-hour flight to Dallas was of the best kind—completely unremarkable. Rob had booked late, so they traded his usual First Class seat for an aisle in the back cabin. Hey, Rob thought, at least it's not a middle seat next to the lav. His former secretary had arranged for an Avis SUV and a room at the airport Marriott. It was over an hour up to Sherman, better driven in the daylight. Rob checked in, then got on the internet to check his email. He was pleased that, along with the contact info for 'Eder Holguin,' JR had included an unredacted copy of the affidavit filed by Sandra Smith, back in November 1981, detailing her activities and claims related to the Menese operation in and around San Francisco. It made for interesting reading, but no mentions of Bolinas or anything else that would help Rob make sense of the case he was on. Still, more is always better than less.

Rob left early for Sherman. The Dallas traffic is a bear, and he wanted to avoid what he could. After clearing the northern loop of the freeway and getting on to Highway 75, it was clear sailing. Lots of Dallas-bound traffic, but northbound was easy travelling. With a stop for breakfast at a Love's truck stop, the drive was around two hours. For a place to meet the man now called Eder Holguin, he wanted to follow his tried-and-true approach. He cruised around until he saw a cop parked on the street, pulled up and rolled down his window.

"Mornin' Brother," Rob was smiling, "hoping you can give me a bit of guidance."

The cop noticed the inflection on the word 'Brother,' "You on the job, buddy?"

"Used to be. Twenty years of service to our Federal Government. But right now, I'm just looking for the oldest café in town—assuming it's safe to eat the food and drink the coffee!"

The local cop laughed, "That'll be Lit'l Store Hamburgers, over on South Rusk. Take a right at the second light down. And before you ask, yes, they have more than hamburgers—and the coffee is the best in North Texas!"

"Copy that," the standard reply between every veteran, cop and first responder, "stay safe out here."

The local cop wasn't lying—the coffee was outstanding. The place was old school cool, and the waitress was fast and friendly. Rob had called Holguin, on his way to the place, arranging to meet there. He walked in about ten minutes after

Rob. The two men made eye contact, and Eder joined Rob at his table. On the way, he was acknowledged by the folks at three other tables. Obviously, a well-liked guy, thought Rob.

"Mr. Anderson?" asked the man called Eder Holguin.

"That's me, but please, call me Rob."

"Eder," the man replied, "pleased to meet you. I hope I can be of some help. That said, I don't think we want to get to deep, inside here."

"Sure, I get it." Rob understood the risks that every Witness Protection participant lived with. "Let's have a cuppa Joe and you can tell me about life here in Sherman, TX."

For the next half hour, Eder told Rob about his 'new life' as a citizen and businessman in small town Texas. He had—through the help of 'friends'—secured a Ford dealership in town. He sponsored a Little League team and was a Deacon at St. Mary's Catholic Parish. A pillar of the Community. Rob suggested they take a ride, to get to the heart of why he wanted to meet in the first place. The former drug dealer suggested a nearby park, where they could sit and have a quiet conversation, so that's where they went.

"First off, you see what I have here," said Eder, "I've worked hard to turn my life around and to become a solid citizen. Please promise me you won't fuck that up."

"I've got nothing but respect," came the reply. "You're doing the right things. I wish every person we helped had done the right things, but that's certainly not the case. I'm only here to learn what I can and then get on my way."

"Then we are cool. As you know, I wasn't born as 'Eder Holguin'—nor am I of Mexican descent, but Nicaraguan. My birth name is Jorge Menolos Cantarerro. I'm the son of Jairo Menolos and nephew of Norwin Menolos. I know you know those names."

Rob did, indeed. "Quite the pedigree. I can see why you might want to leave all that behind. What I want to know is about the house in Bolinas. The one where the Colombian, Flores was murdered," Rob pulled out the pictures taken by Harker and James, "particularly about this day and these pictures, from 1979. This is you, right?" he asked, pointing to a somewhat different looking young man.

"Yes sir, that WAS me. As you can tell, a few things are different," Eder stroked his bald head with a smile, "and not just on the outside. And yes, even though it's been twenty-six years,

I remember that day. But mostly I remember the days right after that day," Rob could see the flash of memories in the other man's facial expressions, "especially after seeing these photos. No one ever asked me about the dude from New Orleans. As far as I know, no one had any interest at the time. But, man, he was pissed about the two freaks taking pictures. Flores just blew it off as they were just two dumbass hippies from farm country. Two dumbass hippies who just had an extensive network for moving product. Flores said he'd been doing business with them for a while and that they were cool. Still, he made the guys give him their cameras before they left. Drugstore disposable pieces of shit. Looks like they must have kept one from him."

"So it would seem," Rob nodded, "tell me more about the guy from New Orleans and the next few days."

"Right. As I told you, no one thought much about the fellow—I think his last name was Freschette or a name like that. He was an associate of my uncle, Norwin. My dad was also there. He and Flores were calling the guy 'Woody'—like the Toy Story guy –it was some kind of inside joke," Holguin continued, "anyway, he was pissed off bad. For the next couple of days, he was like, 'if anything comes of this, I promise you, heads will fucking roll!' shit like that. Flores and my dad finally got him calmed down, but he wasn't in a great mood up until the day he left. One other thing, there was plenty of discussion about the CIA and the DEA at this meeting. I didn't think it was unusual, because my father and uncles are always talking about working with both those groups. I never knew how much was truth and how much was bullshit. Still, the Menolos family always seemed to get away with some outrageous shit, so I wouldn't blow it off. The dude from New Orleans was trying to get the Menolos group to switch suppliers to the Cali Cartel, from Medellin. Offered us better quality and better prices."

"All right, amigo, you've been more helpful than you know," Rob stood. "I'll leave you to this fine new life you've built here. And good luck to your Little League team!"

The men shook hands and walked together back to where they'd parked. Rob figured he had enough to let him start his investigation down in the Big Easy. First though, before rushing directly into unknown territory, he wanted to get back to DC, where he had solid government contacts to leverage. He had plenty of research to do, covering twenty-five years of dead space. On his walk back to the car, Rob thought, man, it's 10:30 in the morning and already 85 degrees. How can anyone love August in this part of the country?

Chapter 19—Sharpening the Saw

Rob got back to his Georgetown apartment late in the day, on August 27th, 2005. His plan was to research anything he could find on 'Freschette' on the New Orleans area, via the internet and though his remaining government sources. What he was able to search out on the internet was quite impressive. Turned out the one Dante Freschette was a scion of the well-known lumber dynasty. A nephew of a nephew, or some such relationship.

The history of the empire began in the latter part of the 19th century with the efforts of the patriarch, Francis Freschette, who was ready to take advantage of the opportunity afforded by the building of new railroads westward into Texas. He slowly acquired thousands of acres of cypress-bearing swampland in Louisiana and began a timber harvesting and milling operation. The Freschette Cypress Company became one of the largest lumber companies in the United States by the early 20th century. As time changed, they sawed their last log in 1934. As luck would have it, they discovered oil and gas on the former cypress lands in the early 1930s, opening a new chapter in the organization's history. And generating a significant revenue stream, resulting in significant family wealth. The Freschette family also became well-ensconced in Louisiana politics, thanks to generous donations to the right people at the right times.

All he could learn about the details of Dante Freschette's development were sparse, at best. Dante graduated from Loyola in 1972, which would make him close to Rob's age. He used his business degree and his family money to launch his own venture, called Exotic Wood Imports Corporation, importing lumber from Central and South America, through the port of New Orleans. He owned a fleet of freighters and cargo aircraft, used for transporting the lumber north and returning south with 'humanitarian supplies' under contract to the United States Agency for International Development and a couple of private non-profit humanitarian assistance organizations. Dante Freschette was still a respected member of New Orleans High Society, as far as Rob could determine.

Rob also found an interesting reference to 'lumber' and 'New Orleans' in the CIA's Office of Inspector General's report on the allegations that CIA had been in bed with Menolos and others, back in the heyday of the Iran-Contra Affair. A DEA informant had told them that cocaine was being brought into New Orleans in hollowed out lumber from Ecuador. The most interesting discovery was that there was no mention of Dante Freschette, or Exotic Wood Imports Corporation, in the report—

even though Freschette's company was the single largest importer of such lumber. No charges were ever brought against Dante. His warehouses, airplane nor boats were never raided or inspected. Something stinks, Rob thought, time to pull in a few past-due debts.

The next morning, Rob called Kevin McMenimen first, to touch base on his progress so far. Kevin was well-connected with his friends at the FBI and worked with them regularly on retail crime mitigation operations. Rob currently felt like the FBI was the only remaining federal agency worthy of being trusted—and he wasn't all that sure about them, either.

"How about having some of your cohort investigate this guy Dante Freschette, for me? Nothing top secret, just references, known associates, current situation, like that," Rob expected little, but had to ask, "I'll forward over what details I have."

"I'll make a few calls. Are you planning to go down to N'awlins?" Kevin asked, with a terrible attempt at a Southern accent. "They have a major hurricane heading their way—you may want to pay close attention to that."

"Yeah, I've been watching the Weather Channel—damn thing is near Category Five! Looks wicked and it's supposed to hit in a couple of days. For the life of me, I can't figure out why anyone would want to live below sea level."

On the morning of August 29th, the news from New Orleans was dire. Hurricane Katrina had done extensive damage to the levee systems, causing massive flooding in the city. The airport was closed. Access to the city was restricted to First Responders—cops, military and medical teams. It was clear that Rob would not be going to Louisiana in the immediate future. He focused his efforts on learning everything he could about Dante Freschette and his ties to cocaine—and his probable ties to the CIA. Based on what he already had, related to the smuggling and the relationship with the Menolos organization, Rob wasn't ready to write off anything. He reached out to another former protégé at the Drug Enforcement Administration.

Kathy Sheetz had been an up-and-coming agent, towards the end of Rob's career. She had excelled in all the classes Rob taught and was an especially good undercover operative, and a seriously good practitioner of Kempo Karate. She spearheaded an operation in Omaha, dubbed 'Operation Snow White,' in which she'd brought down a group that included two commercial airline pilots and a prominent real estate broker. That success, along with her top-shelf professionalism, had earned her the title of Deputy Director at the new Quantico Headquarters of the DEA.

"Hey, Snow White, Frank Dean calling!" Rob knew those names would get a laugh. "How's about a sandwich and coffee with an old pal?"

Deputy Director Sheetz chuckled, "Rob, you old asshole! How's the toughest teacher I ever had? I'd make time for you, any day!"

"That's great! But I warn you in advance, I'm going to ask you for a favor. Just not over the phone," Rob tried not to sound paranoid, "Can we do tomorrow afternoon?"

Rob had struggled through a few romantic relationships in his life, but never had the urge for anything serious. He had, though, always thought that Kathy Sheetz was a woman that could change all that. Unfortunately, for the first years after they first met, in one of his Forensic Accounting classes at the Training Facility, professional decorum wouldn't allow him to do anything about it. Later, Kathy had been assigned half-way across the country, then she had subsequently gotten married to a Navy SEAL. Timing was everything.

"Great to see you, Rob," Kathy said, with a polite kiss on the cheek, "it's been far too long!"

"Yes, Ma'am, it sure has," Rob thought she was as gorgeous as ever, "life has its way with folks like us, doesn't it? You look terrific—you are definitely not spending all your hours behind that corner office desk!"

With a playful gleam in her eyes, the tall brunette DEA Deputy Director replied, "Being there at Quantico has its benefits. They have a super gym, fitness trails—and I've been training in Krav Maga alongside the FBI trainees. You're looking pretty svelte yourself, for an old guy," a wink came with this, "still training in Taekwondo?"

"You bet. I've recently been promoted to 8th Degree Black Belt. Officially a Grandmaster, for what that's worth!" Rob was very proud of this accomplishment, and he didn't try to hide it. Lots of blood, sweat and tears went into that—and not only HIS blood.

"Oss," she replied, with the universal utterance of martial arts respect, "That is damn cool! I guess I should bow to you, next we meet—and I hope that happens sooner than later! For now, though, my time is tight. You didn't just invite me here for a turkey & Swiss sandwich. What can I try to help you with?"

Rob gave the Reader's Digest version of the case he was running. Some he figured she already knew, but he wanted to judge her reaction to a few of the names and scenarios he was working with. She showed him nothing.

"Where I am now is, I need to get as much as I can on this guy Freschette, what DEA knows about him—and what they probably don't want anyone to know they know. What's his connection, if any, with our friends in Langley? I'm convinced there is a connection, by the way, whether or not they'll own up to it. You and I both know that there are no coincidences, but if there were, this case would be the poster child."

"The name doesn't ring any bells, but certainly connections do. And I put nothing past the CIA. There's even a strong case to be made for their direct involvement in the Camarena murder. We know very well what Ollie North and his merry band were doing for the Contras. The worst part, from my personal perspective, was the likely involvement of DEA in that crap. Things have changed a lot in both CIA and DEA over the past 20 years, but you can be sure there's a rug someplace with an enormous lump of garbage swept beneath it. I'll see what I can do for you," with that, Kathy stood—and held that farewell kiss on the cheek a beat longer than customary, "let's have dinner next time. My treat."

Rob was all smiles on his ride home. That meeting turned out great, even if Kathy delivered nothing about Dante Freschette, Rob thought. Although he hoped it did. The day was young, so on his way home from Quantico he paid a visit to one of his Taekwondo mentors, Grandmaster Jhoon Rhee, in DC. Nothing like a great martial arts workout to get the juices flowing. He had known and trained with Grandmaster Rhee since being reassigned to Washington in 1980. Jhoon Rhee was known as "The Father of American Taekwondo." He gave special private training to elite law enforcement professionals and certain other government operatives. No 'tournament style fighting' in these classes. Every movement was with martial intent—meant to disable, maim, or kill an opponent. The man was 75 years old, with cat-like reflexes and seriously hard kicks and punches. Rob felt the need to hone his knife fighting and defensive skills. He spent four hours in Grandmaster Rhee's private studio and felt good about the outcome. He showered off the well-earned sweat, bowed deeply to the Grandmaster, and headed home to Georgetown. At that moment, Rob didn't realize just how timely those lessons would prove to be.

On the morning of September 2nd, Rob heard the Mayor of New Orleans all but crying for help, over the radio. The City had gone to hell, according to all reports. Chaos is the only word that fit. Rob's contacts were of no help at the local level because they had all either already been on a Labor Day vacation or had evacuated prior to the landfall of Hurricane Katrina. Now, they could not get back in and couldn't function if they had. Nothing to do but wait things out and keep digging for more information. The 'Big Easy' was definitely not very easy at the moment.

On the morning of September 6th, though, fate began her sultry dance. Rob's first call that morning was from Deputy Director Kathy Sheetz.

"Mornin' Rob, ready for some good news / bad news?"

"Well, hello," Rob answered, "first off, regardless of what the news is, I honestly appreciate the effort. Now, pick one and let's hear it."

"It's all good, my friend, glad to help you. And I hope this call ends with a dinner invitation! I'll start with the good news: it turns out that Dante Freschette has quite a folder over here. The bad news: the information is sealed and heavily redacted. If it wasn't for my status, it could not have been accessed at all. My personal conclusion is, you're right about his involvement with trafficking and his relationship with a certain group of shady characters from Langley. The first records date back to 1979 with suspicions of using his planes to fly guns to the Contra rebels, based in El Salvador. Suspicions were also high that those planes were not returning empty, if you get my drift. Nothing developed because investigations were squelched by another federal agency, the name of which is redacted in the Form DEA 6."

"Wait," Rob was incredulous, "NOBODY changes a Form 6, once it's filed, right? If they redacted it, then there was a much bigger game afoot, no?"

"Oh, not just a single Form 6—ALL the Form 6's!" Sheetz sounded exasperated, "I've only seen a few, ever, and those always explained away as 'in the interest of National Security.' We last saw that in those filed by Special Agent Hector Berrellez, in the Kiki Camarena murder investigations. Filing those reports cost Berrellez his Supervisor role in the investigation and got him reassigned to a desk in DC. They did not place the reports into the records that we can see. I knew Hector, so I absolutely trust that those Form DEA 6's were actually submitted. I'm sure we'd get the same song and dance here, as well."

"There are some usable nuggets, though," she continued, "We have addresses for Freschette's houses and offices, as recently as 2001. Substantial places, so my guess is the data is still valid. I'll get you all that, but I have to ask: what's your game plan?"

"I could tell you, but then…" Rob couldn't hold the dark tone without laughing, "honestly, I'm not sure. I know this, though. I plan to have an in person chat with this good old boy, to clear up what I can about two murders, twenty-five years back. Don't ask me why because I don't have a worthwhile answer. Closure, I guess. Even the murderers of two dipshit dealers deserve to be outed. How about you deliver the findings to La Chaumière, say 8PM? Assuming you like French food."

Deputy Director Sheetz did not hesitate, "Ooo la la! I love that place and that food. You are on, with one condition. Dinner in Georgetown tonight; breakfast in Foggy Bottom, in the morning."

"Breakfast? I'm in. Where in Foggy Bottom?"

"My apartment," came the soft reply, "unless you're a complete idiot, you'll still be there."

The second call Rob received that morning was from Kevin McMenimen.

"Rob, this call falls into the 'you can't make this shit up' category. If you really want to get right to the heart of things in New Orleans, I think I just found you a way in. I got a call last night from a guy I met at a loss prevention conference awhile back. He was speaking about the potential impact of disasters on the US supply chain. Smart guy. Anyway, his name is Ken Fisher, and he's one of your former Ranger brothers, did two tours in Nam. I think he said he went over in 1970. Regardless, he's in New Orleans, working directly with the leadership of the city, restoring command and control."

Kevin continued, "He reached out to me because he knows my FBI background and of the work we've done in addressing retail organized crime and loss prevention. He is aware of some sketchy shit going on, being organized by a few of the Mayor's first-tier cadre. He says these guys, including several cops, are doing nightly raids on the incapacitated retail establishments around their hotel. Says it started small, just to secure clean duds for the staff. That's why they were all dressed alike in some of the pictures being printed in the papers. Now, according to Fisher, a few of these guys are branching out."

"How do I fit in?" Rob asked, though he thought he already knew the answer.

"We can work on the details, but here's what Ken and I discussed. You can come in under his organization—he's currently with a large systems integration company—but not actually put on his payroll. No one else will know that part. He has an open slot for a role working in the Finance Department for the City of New Orleans—they call it NOLA—in helping to organize and account for the claims they plan to make against the massive influx of money the Fed is about to throw at them. Ken thinks that the billions heading their way will be ripe pickings for these pseudo-thugs. His goal is to get some hard evidence before taking this to law enforcement. He has a multimillion-dollar contract at risk, which he doesn't want to blow up, should he be wrong."

"Seems legit. What's the timing and the game plan? More importantly, will I have the opportunity to deal with my actual mission? I mean, you know I'll handle this job, too, but I do want to get after Dante Freschette."

"You'll be in the middle of anyone who is anyone, in the City. These guys down there are, and always have been, all about the *quid pro quo*. If your boy Dante is a player in that part of the world, somebody at City Hall will be in his pocket," Kevin had to chuckle when he added, "Fisher says, 'these guys are too stupid to be successful crooks,' and he's probably right.

If you're in, you need to get down there, ASAP. Fly into Houston—I'll pull some strings with my pals at AVIS to get you a car. They still rave about the work you did for them a couple of years ago. Ken said you should bring your own gun. He also asked that you bring in some other much-needed supplies: Scotch, cigars and Red Man chewing tobacco. That last item is for bartering with the military guys. He'll get you a bunk at the Superdome Grand Hyatt, where they are all sleeping. It's also where the temporary Emergency Operations Center and most of City Hall are headquartered. Don't expect room service. Or running water."

Dinner with Kathy was even better than expected—and he expected it to be great. Breakfast was even more pleasant. Everything that happened in between was beyond description! They had met at the restaurant, exchanged their respective information, then settled in to getting to know each other. They both liked what they learned. The chemistry was strong between them. Back at her apartment, with Weather Report's Sweetnighter on the turntable, and after glasses of a fine Silver Oak cabernet, they consummated a twenty-year mutual desire for each other. They didn't have to wake up before making breakfast.

The next morning, Rob headed back to his townhouse in Georgetown, packed a go-bag with appropriate gear, including satellite phone, BDUs, boots, his favorite Benchmade auto-deploy knife and his field trauma kit. In a locking Pelican case, he packed his Remington-Rand 1911, along with its custom Kramer Leather paddle holster, a Walther PPKS .380 automatic, as his backup gun—everyone needs a BUG, he thought—with ankle holster, extra magazines and five boxes of ammo for each weapon. He was checking his bag to Houston, so none of these would be a problem. His former secretary had made his reservations, and he was excited to be getting mud on his boots. And probably black mold, in this case. Steven Covey once said: 'We are the instruments of our own performance, and to be effective, we need to recognize the importance of taking time regularly to sharpen the saw.' Rob's saw was as sharp as he could possibly make it. He was ready.

Chapter 20—The Big Not-So-Easy

Rob's plane landed in Houston right on time. He secured his checked baggage, discretely checking to ensure that everything was intact. With all being as it should, he headed off to the rental car center, where he picked up his Ford F-150. Once on the road, he used his cell phone to call a number that Kevin had been given him for Ken Fisher, in New Orleans. They had spoken once, before Rob left Washington, DC. Ken seemed like a standup guy, and their relationship as brother Rangers was clearly a plus.

"Yo, Ranger Fisher, how go the campaigns?"

"Ranger Rob!" came the response, "all is as it always is here: Same shit different day. I'm lucky that most of my team have military backgrounds. One other Ranger / Green Beany named Calvin Diggs, too. Good operator and a trusted soul. You'll fit well. Just hammer down on I-10 until you get to Tchoupitoulas Street exit. Take a left and go to Poydras, then another left. Follow that down to the Hyatt. Park on what they call the 'neutral ground' in the middle of Loyola Street. 3rd Brigade—3 Panther—of the 82nd Airborne is here and billeted at our hotel. One of them will be at the door on Loyola—let him know you're with us. Keep your weapons secured—we can't carry openly. Copy all?"

"Roger that. I've picked up the extra supplies you requested—I like the way you think. See you in a few hours!" Rob felt the same anticipation that he always felt before an engagement.

He drove as fast as he reasonably could, sharing Interstate 10 with every kind of truck, carrying loads of emergency relief supplies, all heading East, and seeing busloads of people heading in the opposite direction. It was surreal. Arriving into the outskirts and then the actual city of New Orleans, Rob realized that 'surreal' was the only word that fit. Standing water, along with watermarks on buildings that showed just how high it had been just a day or two earlier. Wind-damaged buildings and destroyed signs along the roadway. More helicopters in the air than he had seen since Nam. Military everywhere and what seemed like every redneck in the South hauling boats to help with what rescue efforts they could. It mingled feelings of awe with feelings of pride—this was how America came together.

Having parked as directed, Rob walked up the steps to the glassed entrance to the Superdome Grand Hyatt. Surely, not so 'Grand' right now, Rob thought. The entire north side of the glass-skinned building had been blown to shreds. He cleared though the security checkpoint, and was directed to the fourth floor, where a temporary Emergency Operation Center was being developed. The trooper at the security desk had told him to 'look for the tall guy in the red ball cap,' which made retired Command Sergeant Major Ken Fisher easy to pick out of the hustle.

"SarMajor, Rob Anderson reporting as requested!" If anyone in the US Army had ever used the full title 'Sergeant Major' in a conversation, Rob was unaware of it. "How may I be of service?"

Fisher stuck out his hand, delivering a firm and solid shake. "Glad to have you here, compadre, we got some shit to clean up! Haul your gear up to room 605—that's our Fort Apache—then get back down here. We need every hand we can get right now. Don't worry about your toys and tools. I have negotiated an arrangement with Captain Nate Albers, 'Six' of the 3 Panther guys. He's a Ranger. We get them Red Man; they make sure no jerk-offs get to our wing of the sixth floor!"

"Sounds like a good swap," Rob grinned. "I'll be back shortly. I'll do whatever you need done, Brother!"

For the next several hours, Rob worked alongside the team that Fisher had assembled from his own company, a company that he'd contracted, and members of the staff of the City of New Orleans, setting up table and chairs. They were working in a large ballroom and still had plenty to do. According to Ken, this had been ongoing for the past 24 hours and would keep going until they were done. It would be the Command Post for the entire Local, State and Federal Response, in NOLA.

At around 8:00 PM, Ken pulled Rob aside and said, "Let's head upstairs. We need to talk before we head over to the 'Club 1660.' You need the lay of the land and a roster of the players."

"Club 1660? There are bars open?" Rob was a bit surprised, but never passed a cold beer and a shot or three.

"Well," chuckled Fisher, "there are, hell some never closed, but that's not where we're going. Room 1660 is where the City's IT Staff—mostly contractors—meet after the action slows down. They all report to the IT Director, who also refers to himself as 'Deputy Mayor,' which word is, he ain't. Commandeered the title, to sound more credible during the response activities. You'll also meet a few cops, construction contractors and private security guys. Every one of them is aware of and has, seemingly, participated in the raids they've been making on high-end stores. 'Sanctified looting' is what I'd call it. I've earned their trust, for the most part, and they've invited me on a few of their 'adventures.' I have graciously declined, due to my advanced years and level of fitness."

"How you got through that last bit of bullshit without laughing, has me amazed," Rob said that while looking at a six-foot- six, 200-pound guy, who looked as if he could re-do Ranger School tomorrow, "all the rest seems interesting though. No worries about bringing me into the mix?"

"No worries, I've already been pumping you up. These pukes are like fan boys when it comes to combat vets. They know you were a Ranger and in-country around the same time I was. Except earlier. Because you're old." Ken didn't even change his expression with that. His ball-busting skills were top of the mark, "I'd be surprised if they don't want to kiss you."

"You're a fucking laugh a minute, eh big guy?" Rob did laugh, though, "I still have a stroke or two in me, before my stroke or two. Any concerns if I wear my ankle rig?"

"I'd be concerned if you don't. They are all packing, somewhere or other. I carry my .357 J-frame in my BDU pocket—and they all know it. I've never felt threatened, but I also don't trust one of them."

'Be polite, be professional, but have a plan to kill everybody you meet,' "Mad Dog Mattis certainly has a way with words, doesn't he? He'd have made a good Ranger," Rob had a glint in his eyes, "and I subscribe to his philosophies."

"HOOAH!" came the response. "Also important—I'm pretty sure that Fred Marfel, He's the CTO—Chief Technology Officer—but calls himself 'Deputy Mayor,' isn't fully aware of the breadth of his team's business activities. He was all-in on the first raids, to secure clean clothing for his folks—hell man, can't blame them for that—but I don't think he knows about the wholesale thefts that are happening. That doesn't make him clean, though. He is gaming the system with contractors, hand over fist. He's made less-than-subtle 'suggestions' to me about who I should put on my payroll. I've let him know I don't roll that way. He's still trying. As for the rest of their 'Cajun Mafia,' you'll know their shit when you see it. As I told Kevin, they're too stupid to be good crooks."

The two aging Rangers spent the next hour reminiscing about their tours in Nam. They both knew some of the same instructors from 'Finishing School' in Nha Trang but had both been in different tactical areas of operation and different units for their actual duty assignments. Still, the work had been the same. There was no Long Range Patrol or Ranger veteran of the war that had not been in numerous firefights and close-quarter combat. After their tours, when Rob had changed courses and ultimately joined DEA, Ken had stayed in the Army for twenty-five years, attaining the rank of Command Sergeant Major in 2nd Ranger Battalion. After he retired, Ken was immediately snatched up by one of the largest defense contractors. His role was to develop and lead an information technology-based disaster response unit. After proving his worth by assisting the Port Authority of New York, after the attacks of 9/11, they made him Global Managing Partner of the business unit. Thus, his involvement here in New Orleans. Both men had led equally impressive lives. Rob knew he had a good wingman in Ken Fisher.

"Here we go, Brother," Ken said, knocking on the door to room 1660, "let the games fucking begin."

A huge, very redneck-looking dude opened the door, "Yo man, who the fuck is this guy?"

"Chill, Jimmy, this is the Ranger brother I've been telling Fred and Dennis about. He's cool. Where's the Man?"

Ken wasted little time talking to Big Jimmy, Fred Marfel's 'bodyguard' and driver. He had already determined how he would eliminate him if need be. "Rob Anderson, meet Big Jimmy." Rob was not impressed.

"Hey man," came a shout from across the room, "bring that muthafucker over here!" Marfel was at a dining table in the suite, playing Hold 'em with four other guys, "always proud to meet another badass Ranger!"

The guys got drinks from a well-stocked bar—booze which had previously been in one of the Hyatt lounges—and pulled up chairs. Ken once again explained that Rob was being brought in to help with the Finance Officer of the City, in filing for the soon-to-be-allocated megamillions from FEMA. Rob told his usual undercover half-truths about his background. Truth that he had his MBA from Georgetown was in Forensic Accounting; lies that he had worked for Arthur Anderson, specifically on the Enron account. The Firm had been accused of overlooking significant sums of money that had not been represented on Enron's books. The Department of Justice later found Arthur Andersen guilty on federal charges that it obstructed justice by destroying thousands of documents related to Enron.

"By the way, no relation to Arthur," Rob Anderson said with a grin, "but it was a great training ground. We learned where to look—and when not to look. I wasn't high enough up the ladder to get my head chopped off by the Feds, but I did need to find new employment. That's how I landed this job." Rob felt that the well-crafted story would be just enough to signal the crooks that he could be an asset. It worked.

"We're pretty selective about who we let in this room," the speaker was a bearded young guy, sitting at the end of the table, "having a friend in the Finance Office would be quite helpful. Assuming you got what it takes."

"I got this," Rob's reply came with dead-on eye contact. He could fake sincerity with the best of them.

"Dennis Clancy," the bearded one said, in way of introduction, "be advised that 'I got this' comes with a special meaning, with us. Words don't mean shit. We have a lot at stake and the outcome could be very nice for all of us. Or not so nice, for some of us. You get my meaning?" His gaze did not leave Rob's eyes.

"I believe I do, amigo," Rob replied. "I do believe that I do. But hey, I just got here. Give me a minute to catch up!"

The guys at the table laughed at that, then got back to their card game. Rob and Ken exchanged a glance and made their way towards the makeshift bar. The room held about a dozen people, with a few more outside the open sliders—there was no air conditioning—on the balcony overlooking the hotel pool. As they turned, the door opened and a very large black man entered, wearing a New Orleans Police Department uniform.

"That's Oneal," Ken said, "He's on the Mayor's Protection Detail. Seems like a standup guy—quite likeable, in fact—but if he's in this room, he's not to be trusted."

"Looks formidable, that's for sure," Rob said, "Makes 'Big Jimmy' look like a pussy. Still, one shot to his knee and he'll be crying like a schoolgirl. That said, the guy looks like the NFL missed a good prospect."

"Don't think I haven't given that one some thought," Ken had that glint in his eye, "funny you should mention knees and the NFL. Oneal was a top-ranked lineman in school. LSU. He was being seriously scouted by every NFL team in the country—until the knee fracture. He was quite chatty about it. Right leg. If you ever must go there, I'd suggest you get out as fast as your get in. If he grabs you, you will be truly fucked!" The two old warriors clinked glasses with a laugh.

Ken broke down a few others in the group: Mark, owner of one of the City's tech contractors, Paul, another City construction contractor, Dwayne, one of Mark's partners, one NOPD Sergeant, two NOPD Officers and a few others that Ken didn't know. He also pointed out three sets of bolt cutters, pry bars and other tools, behind the kitchenette counter.

"They joked about those 'master keys,' last night," Ken said, nodding at the tools, "I don't think they involve everyone here in the raids, but a few have been wearing very clean, very expensive sneakers, lately. They don't go 'shopping' every night, but I can usually tell when that's on the late-night agenda by the huddle-ups. I haven't seen the signs tonight."

"Looks like my old LRRP skills may get refreshed," Rob was grinning, "next time you have the inkling, I think I'll just tag along—at a discrete distance, of course—to see if I can get a handle on how big this is. Now, how about we blow this place and get a drink? I have a couple of bottles of 18-Year-Old Macallan, back in our rooms!"

The next couple of days were quite full. They introduced Rob to his new 'boss,' NOLA's Chief Financial Officer. He was to be assisting with development of FEMA Project Worksheets—the forms used to document the scope of work and cost estimate for projects. They explained to Rob that this form was used to supply FEMA with the information necessary to approve the scope of work and itemized cost estimate prior to funding, and that they must document each project on a separate Worksheet. NOLA would have a lot of Worksheets. That made for ample opportunity for error—which was likely, since no one on the City's staff had ever seen such a form, and for fraud—which was just as likely, for the same reasons.

Kevin had informed his FBI contacts about the work that Rob was doing in New Orleans. Their Field Office in the city was closed, due to storm damage, but they had a team working out of the Monteleone Hotel. They did not, however, have anyone on the 'inside,' and told Kevin that they would welcome the information, if any were to develop. RetailEye Inc. had an ongoing consulting relationship with the Federal Bureau of Investigation, so was a trusted entity with appropriate clearances. But no one trusted anyone inside New Orleans government, with the levels of funds which were about to flow.

The morning of September 11th brought with it an appropriately somber feeling. Four years was not long enough to have lost the sense of pride and anger that bonded every American on that day in 2001. Even the otherwise shady and conniving members of our society were simply Americans on 9/11. They halted work for moments of silence, at 8:46 AM, 9:03 AM, 9:37 AM and 10:03 AM, to commemorate the times of the events of the attack. Rob was pleased that, even amid dealing with a disaster such as Hurricane Katrina, everyone was humbled and respectful on this day.

On his way back to his desk, Rob struck up a conversation with David Wilson, NOLA's Director of Budgets and Planning.

"Rob Anderson," the introduction was accompanied by an extended hand and a smile, "I hoped that my first visit to New Orleans would be under better circumstances!" He lied about this being his first trip—Rob had been to NOLA on two other occasions, while with the DEA.

"Welcome to the asylum," Wilson seemed like a decent guy, "as the Eagles say: 'you can check out, but you can never leave.' I understand you're working on the PWs?"

"Yes, sir. Plenty of work to go around! The folks say you're a lifelong New Orleanian. I was wondering if you knew a guy from here whose cousin I served with in Nam. Last name of Freschette. I think he's in the lumber business?"

"Damn, man, you runnin' with the big dogs! Freschette's are the definition of 'Old Money'—been in the lumber business for over a century. Gas and oil, too. The main man—heir to the throne, so to speak—is Dante Freschette, he's the grandson of the founder. They own about half of Louisiana! Dante is on the Economic Advisory Board for New Orleans—but he's no fan of the current Mayor. I know nothing about any of his cousins, though."

"Holy moly, I had no idea that I was hanging with American Royalty!" Rob put on the show, "any word on how Dante fared through the storm?"

"I understand he has homes in a few places, but in NOLA, he has a mansion up in the Garden District. They did not get any water from the storm, but got some bad wind damage, I understand. Mostly took out a bunch of those beautiful oaks, along St. Charles. Not much home damage reported, though. They discussed some of that in today's executive situation report. Said that some folks up there are back and have brought in private security companies to protect their assets."

"Assets, or asses?" Rob asked with a wink. Both men got a laugh out of that, then went their separate ways. Rob got information, too. He already had the address of the place at 2211 Prytania Street, thanks to Kathy Sheetz, but now he knew

Dante might actually have come back to town—Rob was already planning a visit.

Chapter 21—Night Moves

At the end of his day at City Hall, Rob stopped back at the Emergency Operations Center, on the fourth floor of the Hyatt. The EOC was busy, even at 7:30 pm. Ken Fisher was at his makeshift command center, near the front door. The 'Tall Guy in the Red Hat' was impossible to miss. He was engaged in a conversation with Calvin Diggs, the former Special Forces trooper. Rob gave a wave and walked over.

"Two Rangers, cooking up a plan… somebody's shit is about to be in the breeze!" Rob gave both men fist bumps.

Diggs grinned, "They say three's a crowd, but with Snake Eaters, it's more like 'crowd control!' How you doin', Brother? Finding your way through the bullshit at City Hall?"

"Shit," spoke Ken Fisher, "the fucker's probably running the place already! HOOAH!" The three men had a good laugh over that one.

"It's a clusterfuck, most assuredly, but it's all good," answered Rob. "I'm ready for some chow. Which MREs are we having tonight—Meals Refusing to Exit, or Meal Rushing to Exit?" Another hearty round of laughter ensued, "I'd eat the north end of a southbound water buffalo, right now."

Diggs had just returned from a chow break, so Ken passed command to him, then the two new friends went back to Room 605 for food, a beverage and an update on the day.

"If you need to catch forty winks, do it now," Fisher turned serious, "I think you'll be busy tonight. I'm pretty sure the 'Roving Raiders' will be out and about tonight. I know you want to get some up-close G2 on all that."

"Right on. And I also got some intel on my prime target, too. I need to work up a plan to make a late-night visit to the Garden District. Any thoughts on an approach to that?" Rob would need to get past the patrols of military and law enforcement, enforcing the nightly curfew, "But before I get too far, I want to do a bit of daylight recon. Can you break away for a drive-about tomorrow?"

"We shall make that happen," came the reply. "I'll see you in about an hour to head down to the den of thieves."

"I'll want to bring a few specialty items with me, so I can get busy as soon as they leave for their mission," Rob wanted his 1911, his balaclava and his night vision goggles, "know of a safe place to stash all that while we're inside?"

"We'll take the shortcut through the kitchen. You can stash your gear there. We'll leave before the excursion sets out.

You're on your own, from there. If anything goes south, I can't risk my job—I know you get it. But, if you get in a serious bind, I got your back. I'm tight with Captain Albers of 3 Panther. His boys will bail you out." Rob could tell that Ken wanted in on the fun, but simply had too much at stake.

"All good, Brother. I got this."

Rob crossed the hall to his room. The electricity in the hotel was still intermittent, except in the EOC—generators took care of that—so Rob used his trusty SureFire tactical flashlight to gather his gear: his Remington-Rand 1911 and Kramer Leather holster, Armasight N-15 Gen 2+ HD Night Vision Goggles, his Benchmade auto-deploy knife—he chose that blade instead of the Nam-vintage Ka-Bar fighting knife he'd had since the late conflict in Southeast Asia—and a lightweight 'ninja' balaclava. No need to change his black BDU pants and tactical boots—seemed like everyone down here dressed in 'Tacti-cool' garb, so he would fit right in. He also had his ever-present Walther PPKs on his ankle. Rob put all the tactical gear in a small black ballistic ruck and headed over to link up with Ken.

When the men arrived at 'Club 1660,' the usual krewe was there, with a few additions. One group were huddled together, away from the card table, where Marfel and his cronies were playing.

"Head on a swivel, brother," Ken said quietly, "those are the boys to watch."

"Way ahead of you, man. My Spidey-senses are on overdrive," crooks always seemed like crooks, to Rob.

The man in the group doing most of the talking was wearing an NOPD uniform, with sergeant stripes. One had on military camo BDU pants and an olive drab tee shirt—Louisiana National Guard, Rob figured. The other three were in dressed pretty much alike, in cargo pants and fishing shirts. Must have been a good day in the sporting goods department, thought Rob.

"Wassup, SarMajor?" the guy in the BDU pants asked Ken, "you know you want to come party with us—tonight gonna be the night? It could get interesting! Who's your partner, here?"

"Naw, man, I'll pass. But it's all good. This here is an old Ranger Brother of mine. And I do mean old," Ken was playing it to the hilt, "Rob Anderson, meet Master Sergeant Tony Smith. Rob here's working with us on some things in the Finance Office. If you need an extra hand, maybe he can help?"

"Yeah, can't have that, bro," BDU Guy said to Ken, but looking straight at Rob, "don't know shit about him but what you just told me. Maybe down the road if he proves himself worthy."

Rob returned the man's stare. "For what it's worth, Master Sergeant, I really don't give a happy fuck what you do or what you need. Now, you have about two seconds to de-ass my area. I don't think I like you very much."

A tense heartbeat passed, before the Master Sergeant let out a laugh, "Damn, brother, you alright," he said, "take some balls to call out a man my size! Don't worry, we'll have another time to catch up," he said the last part without a smile.

"I sincerely look forward to it, 'brother,'" Rob said, with special emphasis on the last word.

"Alrighty then, that went well," Ken rolled his eyes. "I can hardly wait to introduce you to somebody new!"

Rob caught glimpses of the group of crooks in his peripheral vision. There were some glances his way and some intentionally loud uses of the term 'that muthafuckah,' but he ignored them. He had violated the first part of Mad Dog Mattis' Mantra—he hadn't been nice to the guy when they met—but he was on track with the rest of it—making a plan to kill them if necessary.

After another hour—and drinking water instead of the Ciroc Vodka that seemed in endless supply—Rob gave Ken a nod and discretely left.

Back in the kitchen, the old Recondo soldier donned his gear, but kept the NVG in his ruck. There was only one way out of the Hyatt North Wing, where 1660 was located, other than the kitchen entry door. Rob locked that door behind him, leaving only the exit that he would be watching. He settled in and he waited. The gathering broke up at around 11:30 PM, with people leaving in small groups or alone. About thirty minutes later, the band of thieves came out. From the shadows of a service closet, Rob could hear them talking as they passed.

"Let's keep our shit tight tonight, gentlemen," Rob couldn't tell who was giving directions, but knew it wasn't the asshole Guardsman he'd had the encounter with. "This is gonna be a big night!"

"Damn skippy! Diamonds and gold, baby, that's what I'm talkin' about!" that voice WAS the Master Sergeant and was followed by the sounds of palms slapping palms and a chorus of "hell yes!" from the others.

Rob fell in behind the group of men, a safe distance back. The hotel hallways were well-illuminated and carried sound well.

They went down the fire stairs towards the lobby—which also held the entrance to the New Orleans Centre Shopping Mall. How convenient, Rob thought, they don't even need to go out on the street. The Mall had almost 100 stores, including a Macy's—a RetailEye client—and the usual collection of mall-based specialty shops, including a couple of high-end jewelry stores. The plan was to do like his LRRP missions in Nam—be very quiet and take copious notes. Like most plans, this one was about to go straight to shit.

The Mall had been partially flooded by the storm, but the water had receded. Any clothing on the first level was clearly ruined, but the jewelry would be good to go. The Mall was off limits to everyone, with NOPD barricades and roving guards protecting the entrances. Not even insurance adjusters had been allowed in, as yet. The second floor was not damaged at all but was still inaccessible by unauthorized persons—or well-connected thieves, like these asshats, thought Rob. The muck on the first floor stank and still had some puddles of stagnant water—with plenty of black mold, Rob was sure of that. It was dark, but some light was coming in through the broken panes of the atrium ceiling, from the light towers at the Dome and at the hotel. Enough light to keep the crooks from detecting me, Rob thought. He was almost right.

"Well, well, who the fuck do we have here?" the voice of the big Master Sergeant was right behind him.

How the fuck did I miss that? Rob thought. Before the bad guy could say more, Rob pivoted to his right and struck BDU Guy in his solar plexus with an elbow strike. With his wind taken away, the National Guardsman staggered back three steps, as Rob squared off with him. Dressed all in black and with his balaclava covering his face, it would be hard for someone who knew Rob to identify him. This guy had only met him once.

The Guardsman collected himself quickly but didn't cry out for his buddies. "I am about to kick your ass," he said this almost in a whisper, because he still struggled for breath. He closed the gap with Rob in the crouch of an experienced fighter.

Rob turned his body to the left, angling for his next attack. He faked a left cross, rotating fully through to deliver a spinning sidekick with his right foot. Rob spun, taking his weight on his left foot—which turned out to be problematic—he slipped on the muck under his feet and went down hard. As luck would have it, that slip saved his life. Coming back at Rob, the Master Sergeant had pulled a formidable Bowie knife from behind his back. He swung hard at the old Ranger—Rob wasn't there to hit.

As he rolled away, Rob saw the glint of the stainless-steel blade in the hands of his attacker. Game on, asshole, he thought. As the big man stumbled from the force of his lunge into thin air, Rob came to his feet, pulling his own knife. As the attacker turned back to him, Rob made three rapid slices—first across the forearm of his opponent's knife hand, severing the tendons to the hand; next, an underhand stroke to the triceps muscle of the same arm, rendering the arm useless for striking or blocking; finally, a downward slice across the man's right quadriceps, just above the knee, taking away his ability to stand or retreat. All in about two second's time. As the Master Sergeant's leg collapsed beneath him, Rob drove his right knee into the man's chin, knocking him unconscious. Not even time for a scream, Rob thought. I still got it! He also gave a silent 'thank you' to Grand Master Jhoon Rhee, for the refresher training he'd been wise enough to take before this mission—he would thank him in person, when he got back home.

While no loud shouts came from either man during their fight, the noise was unmistakable. The other men were calling out— not yelling though, they couldn't afford that noise—and were running back towards the sounds. By the time they got to their fallen comrade, Rob was long gone. Just like in the Nam, Rob thought, leave nothin' but screaming widows and smokin' holes. These assholes have a mess to clean up and some serious explaining to do. Rob planned to give his report to Kevin and the FBI first thing tomorrow. Since there was at least one NOPD Officer and a National Guard Senior Non-Commissioned Officer involved, the Feds could decide how to handle it. But these guys were small time—Rob still had bait in the water for the bigger fish. For now, though, he needed a shower—and he had to get some blood out of his gear. As he walked back to his sixth-floor room, he was singing Bob Segar's 'Night Moves' inside his head—just as he'd done after every stealth mission since the song came out, in 1976.

Chapter 22—Garden District

When Rob came in to the EOC the next morning, Ken Fisher was just heading to grab breakfast.

"C'mon, man—Mother's Restaurant has reopened and they're donating breakfasts to the EOC staff—eggs, grits, bacon, sausage and good ole down-home biscuits 'n' gravy! Makes this old Arkansas boy homesick!"

"I'm all in—except for the grits. I'm originally from Alabama, and ain't never been a grit in my mouth. I'm down for the eggs, sausage and biscuits, though!"

"What! No grits!?! Boy, you need to surrender your Southern Citizenship Card! Sacrilege!" Ken had the perfect look of disgust on his face, "and hey, things got more exciting in the EOC around 'midnight:30.' Seems three or four 'gang members' attacked your pal the NG Master Sergeant, down in the New Orleans Centre Mall. Cut him up good, but not life threatening. That gang-banger was a real artist with his blade. Almost surgical, in fact. Thing is, neither the victim nor his cronies that got him to the medics can explain exactly WHY they were in that off-limits location. NOPD and the MPs are digging in to all that. Weird, huh?"

"Why, yes, that is weird," Rob could never fake incredulity, especially if he knew the actual score, "a little bird told me that the FBI might make a stop by here today, too. Something about 'RICO Act' and 'Conspiracy to Commit Organized Crime.' Who would have suspected upstanding members of our armed forces and police forces to be subject to that?"

Ken handed Rob a Nokia Push-to-Talk phone. "Nextel gave us hundreds of these. Our team is on channel 5. I have a second one that I use to monitor channel 12, which no one else uses. Keep yours on 12—especially if you are off doing that thing you do. Could be that you'll need backup, one of these evenings."

"Gracias, amigo," Rob said with a grin. "One never knows when the cavalry might be needed. Things might get a bit squirrelly over the next week or so. Meanwhile, how about you call me out of the Finance Office at around eleven o'clock, and let's tour the Garden District?"

"I can do that. Be nice to get outside. I have crews working over in the Lower Ninth Ward, too. Tough duty, working with Kenyon on human remains recovery. We can cruise over there when we finish uptown."

The guys wolfed down the best meal they'd had in days, then went on about their business. Rob had called Kevin much earlier, who had the wheels turning with the FBI. He'd conveniently omitted the parts about the hand-to-hand encounter. Plausible deniability was always a good thing, under certain circumstances. Kevin also contacted his Loss Prevention contacts at Macy's letting them in on the investigation. They needed to get a bit more forceful about gaining access to their store, and whatever inventory remained salvageable.

At 10:30, Rob let Wilson know he needed to assist Ken with a project and would be back in a few hours. He met Fisher at his Expedition and they headed uptown. Rob hadn't had an opportunity to get out since his arrival, so was happy for the chance to see the town. The water around the Hyatt was gone by then, with a few standing puddles here and there. The water lines on the buildings told the story of how it had been, though. Some lines were six feet or more above the ground. On some blocks, it looked as if someone had taken a paint roller and left a brownish line all the way from one end to the other. The closer they got to the Mississippi River; the less flooding had occurred. New Orleans is bowl-shaped—the Garden District and Uptown sections were closer to the rim of the bowl. As they turned up St. Charles Street, it seemed like every other house was a mansion, straight out of the 1800s. In many cases, that was absolutely the case. 'Stately' barely did justice to some of them. Though Rob had been to New Orleans a few times, his exposure to the City had been limited to the Central Business District, the Federal Courthouse, Bourbon Street and the hip jazz clubs on Frenchmen Street. Aside from the houses, the thing that really stood out was the abundance of men and women in tactical gear, most carrying some variant of AR-type rifles.

"Are we in fucking Baghdad?" Rob asked.

"Man, you ain't far off the mark," Ken replied, "these guys up here have hired every Woody Rent-a-Cop from here to Canada. Shit man, freakin' Blackwater and Triple Canopy are down here, along with an army of lesser-known companies. There have been a couple of standoffs between these guys and NOPD and the 82nd. One had them both actually aiming their shit at each other!"

"Well," Rob said, "that's freakin' thrilling. I may have my work cut out for me, getting back in here after curfew. I'm really not up for a running gunfight if I can avoid it."

They took St. Charles to 2nd Street, turned left, then left again, onto Prytania Street. Rob wanted a perspective on the neighborhood, so the slightly longer route served him better. 2211 Prytania Street was quite the place. As they approached, it was on their left-hand side and two prominently displayed flags adorned it—one was Old Glory and the other, a flag Rob didn't recognize. It was purple, green and a broad yellow stripe from corner-to-corner, sporting a regal crown, dead center.

"Your buddy was a King of the Krewe of Rex," Ken said, with a bit of surprise in his voice, "that's definitely the Big Leagues around here. That's his royalty flag. King of Rex is always an influential resident involved in civic causes and philanthropy. That does not, however, mean he's not as dirty as a pig's ass. In fact, in this town, it likely means they are. It also means they are very well-connected."

Ken slowed as he neared the private security contractor at the gated driveway. As the guard approached, Ken pointed towards the Humvee at the curb. "Bodyguard and Tactical Security," he read out loud from the Humvee's magnetic logo sign, "where you boys out of?"

"BATS is out of Alabama," the young guy replied, "but I'm from Little Rock. How can I help you gentlemen?"

"Go Razorbacks! I'm from Rogers!" Ken's comment earned him a fist bump from the guard. "We're working at the

Hyatt and just thought we'd check out the damages a bit. Where's Commander's Palace from here? I heard they took a big hit. By the way, this is a cool house, brother. Whose is it?

"Commander's is back yonder way," the Arkansawyer nodded in the general direction of St. Charles Street. "All I know about the owner here is he's a rich sombitch. He was here yesterday, driving a tricked-out Range Rover with snorkel and everything. Brought us all some of those powdery donut things they eat down here. Said he'd be back in a week or two. This ain't a bad gig, man."

Rob leaned over to speak to the security guard. "Where'd you serve? From the way you carry yourself, I'm guessing you weren't Rear Echelon."

"No sir, no REMF here! I was 11Bravo in 25th ID. Two tours in the Sandbox. You guys?"

"Both Regiment guys. I ETS'd after Nam, the CSM here embraced the suck for a bit longer," banter between military guys came with its own language, and Rob loved it.

"Yep, did 25," Ken spoke up, "spent some time attached to the 'lectric strawberry' in Vietnam, but then served in every shithole two-way shooting range they could find. I was there when we started the shit that you got caught up in. We were lasing targets in Desert Storm. My last shit-show was Mogadishu." Ken was understating and Rob knew it. He knew that Fisher had been with Lt. Colonel Lee Van Arsdale and his Delta Team when they attempted to rescue the 'Blackhawk Down,' crew members—Ken had serious combat experience.

"HOOAH!" the young guard was honestly impressed, "you gentlemen stay safe out here!"

"We gotta git," Ken had on his deepest Arkansas accent, "you boys feelin' safe out here? Everything good?"

"Oh, hell yeah. We are locked and loaded, plus there's two more security companies within a block of us, and patrols from the 82nd are past here, every night. We good!" the young guard drew himself to attention and saluted, "pleasure to meet you two heroes!"

"That went pretty well," Rob chuckled. "I think you could have got that trooper to wash your car, if you'd smiled just right. Based on what he said about Freschette's schedule, I have a bit of time to plan this out."

"I already have some thoughts." Ken had that gleam in his eyes that Rob had come to appreciate, "we can discuss it over scotch and a cigar."

Ken and Rob arrived back at the Hyatt at around 1600 hours. The Lower Ninth Ward was a depressing and awesome mess, with homes literally a block away from where they originally stood. Ken's crew there was led by a former Fire Chief, named Jim Cason. Cason reported that three more bodies had been recovered that day and more expected to be found. Ken said it was tough work—it clearly was that. Rob was glad to be a REMF in this operation. During the drive, Rob called Kathy Sheetz to see if she could get him information on the 'BATS' private security company. It took her all of ten minutes to let him know that no such company was licensed in Alabama, Louisiana or Mississippi. That is interesting, he thought, another kettle of spoiled fish to sort through.

After checking in at the EOC and getting a thumbs-up from Ranger Diggs, the two went up to Room 606—Rob's room—to grab a couple of stogies and a bottle of Macallan. They then made their way up to the 27th Floor, to what was once the Regency Club. It was a complete wreck. Not a single unbroken window and only half had yet been boarded up.

"Reserved for us top dogs," Ken laughed, "it's messy, but it's quiet!"

As they smoked and sipped, Ken told Rob what he had in mind. "How would you feel about opening up a bit, to Captain Albers? I think he's more than trustworthy, and it ain't like you'll be asking him to drop a hammer on somebody— although, he might do that for a Brother Ranger, too. I'm thinking he might let you tag along on one or two of his night patrols of the Garden District, if you get my drift."

"Indeed, I do," Rob replied, "if you trust him to that degree, I know I can, too. When can we have a chat?"

"Well, he should walk through that fucked up door, any minute. I assumed that you'd be cool with the idea." Ken raised his glass in a toasted, just as Ranger Albers walked in, "tiiin-hut!" both old soldiers visibly tensed, then broke out in laughter.

"As you fucking were," Albers shouted, "don't over work those ancient knees! Good to see you both!"

Ranger Captain Albers declined the drink offered to him— operational discipline, which both Rob and Ken respected—but accepted the Fuentes Fuentes Opus X cigar. Rob gave him the back story and filled him in on both of his missions. Albers gladly agreed to help Rob infiltrate the Garden District location whenever Rob was ready to rock. He told the guys that he would assign a select group of his soldiers to that patrol—ones that knew the value of discretion and wouldn't make noise about Rob 'disappearing' during the patrol. The three Rangers finished their smokes, looking out over the City of New Orleans. Pretty cool, thought Rob, pretty damn cool.

Chapter 23—Setting the Trap

After a quick, semi-warm shower—Rob had learned from the others in Ken's team to place bottles of water in the windows, to heat up during the day, because the hot water still wasn't working—and grabbing another decent meal, provided by Mother's, he connected with Ken for their nightly visit to the Club 1660. He figured this one might get interesting, based on the adventures of the night before. He wasn't wrong.

As the two entered room 1660, it was obvious that something was different. The only people there were Marfel and his closest team members, all sitting around the dining / poker table. There were no cards. They all looked at the two newcomers and waved them to the table.

Marfel began, "There was some unusual action around here last night—you heard?" Marfel was a white guy, but always seemed to speak with the inflections of a black New Orleanian, "One of our buddies got pretty fucked up. Probably got legal issues comin' too."

Ken spoke first, "Report said some gangbangers jumped him, down in the Mall. Sounds like one of his 'adventures' went haywire, eh?" Everyone knew about the 'scrounging missions,' as they called them, even if they didn't know the full scope of them. Rob remained silent.

"I spoke with him," it was Dennis Clancy who spoke next, "he told me it was one guy, dressed all in black, wearing a ski mask or something," then, looking straight at Rob, "I guess our FNG here knows nothing about that, do ya, brother?" The word 'brother,' was dripping with sarcasm.

Rob stared back and answered, "I may be a 'Fucking New Guy' to you, 'brother,'" Rob mimicked the sarcastic inflection on the word, "but this ain't my first rodeo. I don't know shit about this situation and don't actually give a flying fuck. That dude pissed me off last night, but I didn't fuck him up. If I had, it would have been face-to-face, so that he remembered who did it. I need this work. I will not screw it up over some pussy from the National Guard."

"Chill, boys, chill!" Marfel tried to ease things up, "we have important things to discuss! Our boy Rob here is about to earn his keep!"

Marfel told the group that he was submitting invoices to the Project Worksheet process for a city-wide wireless surveillance camera contract. He had awarded the contract to Mark St.

Pierre's company, without the usual bid process, under 'emergent conditions.'

"We are about to royally screw the current vendor," Marfel said, "and we've got Dell on board with us! This one gonna make us faaat!" He dragged out the word 'fat,' as if he was born in the ghetto.

His directions to Rob were to make sure the multimillion dollar initial invoice made it on to the first PW, no matter what. This was exactly what Rob had been working to uncover—a case of criminal conspiracy to commit fraud. He just needed to knit together a few more details and have evidence of money being transferred, but the FBI would be very interested in what was already on the table. Things were rolling in the right direction for Rob—but the wrong direction for the City of New Orleans.

Dennis chimed in, "Let's be clear, you're still on probation, amigo. So far, you've done nothing to gain our full trust. Tomorrow, bring us a copy of the PW update for the day. I want to see it in writing."

"Too easy. I'll bring you a copy of the update sheet, but it's not ready to be filed to the Feds, just yet." Rob would also make damn sure that submission went to a Federal Agency other than FEMA, however.

"Yo," Ken chimed in, "what about payment for the work my team and I have been doing? We've been here since day three, brought in fifty contractors, worked our asses off and haven't seen shit from NOLA. My ass is in a sling if something doesn't give—and soon."

Marfel glared at Ken, then replied, "Man, y'all are doing great work. I got your contract approved, and I'm looking at more opportunities for you. You just need to get a little better at playing the game, brutha!" I cannot stand this fucker, Rob thought, I hope it's not as obvious as I feel like it is.

Dennis again, "Dude, if you recall, we 'recommended' for you to hire Bobby Davis' company for the administrative work—you brought in outsiders. What the fuck?" The word 'recommended' was accompanied by fingers making the sign for quotation marks.

"The fucking guy just got out of prison on a corruption conviction! My headquarters has a large legal and contracts group, man—they check that kind of shit. I'm not losing my job over anything you 'recommend,' let's keep that straight!" Ken Fisher—all six foot six, 200 pounds of him, was pissed off and on his feet.

Rob stood up beside Ken, left foot on the chair he had just been sitting in, ready for whatever came next. If it was retreat, he was more than ready to leave. If it was a fight, his right hand would draw the Walther from his ankle holster before anyone could stop him.

"Damn, you boys are feisty tonight!" Marfel laughed. "Y'all need some more Ciroc!"

Rob spoke next, "Sorry boys, but this old man needs his beauty sleep. I hope we have a chance to continue the discussion on another day." Rob had eyes locked with Dennis Clancy. "Y'all have a nice night now, ya heah?" spoken in his intentionally worst rendition of a Southern accent.

Rob and Ken walked back to the EOC on the fourth floor. Getting a thumb's up from the night shift supervisor, they took the elevator up to six. It was still relatively early, so the men went to Rob's room for a night cap and a debrief.

"Two things," Rob started, "first, if I don't kill the motherfucker first, I intend to take that punk Clancy down, hard. You're my corroboration—he just admitted to a criminal act. Timing is everything, though. I want to get more info on how high this goes, then pop the lot of them. Next, I saw your contract and invoice in the office today. The contract had an

'Approved' stamp on it. The invoice didn't. I think you need to have a bit of a stronger chat with Fred Marfel—assuming that idiot is actually in charge of anything."

"He's playing games with me. You heard them—they want me to hire their 'recommended' contractors, so they can get their kickback money. They know it isn't coming from my company—we are squeaky clean," Ken sipped his Macallan, "man, I've had our IT people save copies of every email, every spreadsheet and every document that's flowed between us and the City. We've been in CYA-mode since the day we showed up. But you're right, I need to press this. Patience is not a virtue that my corporate finance team is known for. With end-of-month coming up, they want to see cash flowing."

The next day, Rob made calls to his FBI contacts. He was working with the Special Agent in Charge of the Houston Office, James 'Jay' Bowden, because all NOLA ops had been moved there. Also, because no one trusted anyone who worked in NOLA, before the storm—not even the FBI. After explaining what had occurred the night before, and the 'request' to bring Marfel a copy of the PW entries, showing the contract for surveillance cameras, Rob asked for approval to make the bogus entry. Rob wasn't about to forge a federal document without some air cover. The Houston SAC gave him the okay to produce a PW, as requested, which would be seen by the right eyes in NOLA. When the final Project Worksheet was sent up, Marfel, St. Pierre, Clancy, and probably a few others would be 'sent up' at the same time. A new spin on the 'reverse sting' concept that Rob was very familiar with.

When he got to his desk, the surveillance camera invoice—stamped 'Approved'—was on top of the stack that they assigned him to enter in today's batch. Someone in this office is in on the game, Rob thought. Along with the hefty stack of Approved invoices, he also took Ken's invoice from the Pending box. He had a plan.

After a lunch break, Rob placed a copy of the PW entry sheet into a manila envelope, along with the unapproved invoice from Ken Fisher. He made an excuse to leave for a while and made his way from the seventh floor of City Hall to the ninth floor, where Marfel's office was. He knocked and entered to find Marfel and Big Jimmy, his so-called bodyguard, shooting the breeze about football.

"You a Saints fan? That's mandatory, in this town!" Marfel waved his hand toward all the Saints paraphernalia in his office.

"Always been a Bears fan, myself," Rob never denied that loyalty, even in the worst of seasons. "It's not always easy. But, hey, they don't call your team 'the Ain'ts' because they win all the time, right?"

"Yeah, you right!" big Jimmy was chuckling, "but we gotta stay loyal to the boys! They won for us the other night!"

"What you got for me, man? The PW, I do sincerely hope!" Marel had his hand outstretched.

"That, and one other thing—Ken Fisher's invoice. You really need to approve it. I'll be glad to hand-carry it back to Finance." Rob kept eye contact with Marfel, but was also tracking Big Jimmy with his peripheral vision.

"Who the fuck do you think you are, hoss? You comin' up in here tellin' me what I 'need to do"—what am I, your bitch now?" the CTO was on his feet now. So was Big Jimmy.

"I'm telling you that if you don't, Fisher is going to get pulled out of here by his bosses, for mismanaging the project— which you know isn't the case. He's pulled your asses out of the fire a hundred times. He has also covered your ass, just as many times," Rob stood casually, but had his moves sorted out, if it came to that, "Number one, you don't want fresh eyes and a new attitude in here, do you? I don't think so. Number two, while Ken is definitely a trustworthy guy, you're fucking with his livelihood. He's not a guy you want to piss off. Payback is a motherfucker."

Marfel sat back down. Big Jimmy didn't.

"You make an excellent case, Anderson," Marfel said, after a minute with his eyes shut, "and seein' as how you got my special request accomplished, I'm gonna throw y'all a bone. But ain't nothin' free, ole buddy. I have a few more things for you to help me with over there in Finance. I'll let you know, when I'm ready, "he signed Ken's hefty invoice and slid it back across the desk, "now, get the fuck out of my space!"

Rob turned to leave, and Big Jimmy sidestepped to stand directly in his path. Rob stepped right, then juked to the left. Big Jimmy moved to his left but was faked out by Rob's sudden reversal. As he tried to correct, Rob hooked his right foot inside Jimmy's right foot, then rotated his right knee into the fat man's right knee, causing it to buckle. Jimmy stumbled backwards, crashing down hard into a chair.

"Oh, man," Rob said, with mock concern, "you okay there, big guy? That was a weird accident—I bet we couldn't do that again if we tried too!" Rob knew, however, that he could execute that 'leg bite' technique at will. It had served him well in many close-quarter situations. "You need a hand getting up?"

"Fuck off!" Big Jimmy would never admit that he'd been had. "I just lost my balance. Now get out of here, like the man said, before I get pissed and fuck you up!"

Rob smiled his best 'any day, asshole' smile, and proceeded out the door. He walked straight to David Wilson's office in Finance.

"Mr. Wilson, I just ran in to Fred Marfel. He asked me to get him the invoice from Fisher, so that he could approve it. It's right here, ready to go on the PW," Rob handed the envelope to an incredulous Wilson.

"But he told me… yeah, whatever, if the man says do it, we do it," Wilson was shaking his head, "submit it." Rob now knew who was in the pocket of the connivers from Club 1660.

On his way back to his desk, Rob stopped by the machine to photocopy the newly Approved invoice. Ken will smile tonight, Rob thought. And he had set the trap to take down the bad actors who were taking advantage of America's worst natural disaster, to feather their own shitty nests.

Chapter 24—Recon

"Captain Albers, can I have a word?" Rob had stopped by the Hyatt conference room, which billeted 3 Panther of the 82nd Airborne. "I have a special request."

"What can I do for you, Ranger Rob?"

"I'd like to do a dry run with your night patrol of the Garden District this week. It's already the 20th of the month. My target is supposed to be back between now and the end of September. I want to recon the area to see what I can see," Rob replied, "maybe take a few pictures."

"Hooah. How about tonight?" Albers is a solid trooper, Rob thought.

Rob connected with the 3 Panther Staff Sergeant responsible for leading the night patrol, at around 9:00 PM—2100 hours, in military-speak—they would take a 'deuce & a half' to the Walmart Supercenter parking lot, then do foot patrol up Jackson Street to St. Charles, returning by zig-zagging trough the historic Garden District. They positioned Rob in the center of the patrol column, leaving the 'official' troops in front and rear. All the troops had their NVG affixed to their helmets—Rob had his, as well. With the lights deployed by the various private security operators, those appliances would probably not be needed, Rob thought. He wished they were. His job would be so much easier, in complete darkness.

As they approached 2211 Prytania Street, however, Rob's spirits lifted. Apparently, the BATS guards had no large generator-powered light towers, like some of the other homes. The guards wore headlamps, and the house had a few strategically placed floodlights, which were apparently either solar powered or powered by the house's generator. Plenty of darkness, especially on the east side of the house. When the patrol came abreast of the house, Rob saw a very nice Range Rover with the engine running. The driver was chatting with a security guard with captain's bars on his epaulettes. The driver's face was well-illuminated by the captain's headlamp. It was most definitely Dante Freschette. Older, sure, and with a bald head instead of long hair, but the man's features were unmistakable. That French nose was hard to hide. Rob couldn't do anything about it. Not now, not tonight. He's back early, Rob thought. When the patrol got back to the Hyatt, Rob learned exactly why.

It was midnight by the time Rob walked into the EOC. It was usually at least somewhat calm by this time—but not tonight.

Ken, Diggs and their entire team were at the Control Center Desk.

"What's up?" Rob asked. "This can't be good."

Ken looked up, "It's about to get a bit more interesting," he said, "ever been through a hurricane? We've got another storm in the Gulf and it looks like she's coming to NOLA. Rita is shaping up to be a bad bitch. Governor Blanco has issued a state of emergency for all parishes in the southwestern region of Louisiana and has requested a federal state of emergency for the entire state. Refugees still at the New Orleans Convention Center and Superdome are now being evacuated as a precaution, and national guard troops and other emergency personnel in for the Hurricane Katrina aftermath are being mobilized to evacuate. The Mayor will issue a mandatory evacuation for New Orleans, probably before daybreak."

"Well, shit," was the best Rob could come up with to say, "what happens with this place," waving his arms at the EOC, "is everyone outa here?"

"Nope. Not everyone. We will keep a skeleton staff here, including myself. Same with the 82nd. That's why this meeting—I have asked for a small team of volunteers. The rest are being sent over to board a Carnival cruise ship, along with a bunch of non-critical city staff. You should probably consider joining them."

"Screw that!" No way Rob was bailing out, "If you'll allow it, I want to stay. You know I'll be an asset. Besides, I may want this story in my memoirs, some day!"

"You, sir, are nuckin' futz," Ken slapped Rob on the shoulder, "if you're foolish enough to stay here, below sea-level, in a partially destroyed hotel, during a major hurricane, I guess I'm stupid enough to keep you. Frankly, every one of my team members had said the same thing. Rock stars, one and all. Can't have that, though—I need somebody left alive to identify our bodies!" Rob could see that Ken was only half-joking, with that last comment.

The next two days were a scramble. The Mayor did, indeed, declare a mandatory evacuation for New Orleans, resulting in a rapid but orderly exodus of most of the EOC staff. FEMA, military, and all but essential police and firefighters. Rob, Ken, Diggs and a few others manned posts in the EOC to monitor radio traffic and weather reports. The 82nd also left a skeleton force, providing security for the Hyatt-based nerve center of the recovery efforts. As for Rob, all he could think about was how close he had come to Dante Freschette and wondering how long it would be until his next opportunity.

"Ken, let's take a ride," Rob said, "I'd like to get another pass by Prytania Street."

"I suppose we can do that," came the reply. "Probably be good to ensure that those rent-a-cops are following the evac orders. That's as good an excuse as any other."

The men drove to the Garden District and found Ken's homeboy at this station, in front of Freschette's house.

"Yo, troop," Ken said to the guard, "y'all getting out of town, soon?"

"No Sir. The Boss has me and two others on orders to hunker down and stay the course," the Arkansas boy turned his head and spit tobacco juice onto the sidewalk, "I am not thrilled."

"Yeah, well, you'll be less thrilled if this bad bitch comes up in here," Ken had no humor in his voice, "but you gotta do what you gotta do. Just be advised that we will not be sending the cavalry to save your asses!"

"Copy that," the former soldier replied. "The owner of this place was here last night. He said that this house has stood here for over 100 years, with no flooding and no damage worse than a few shingles off the roof. He figures we'll be safe enough."

Here was Rob's opening. "So, what's he doing? He riding it out inside there, too?" That would be just too good to be true, Rob thought.

"Oh, hell no, he said he's heading to Charleston. Said he'd be back when this mess is over. Must be nice to have a private jet, man," the man shook his head, "fuckin' rich bastard!"

"I hear that!" Rob was not pleased, but he knew he had to wait it out. "We'll check back in with you, after we see what Rita brings us. Stay safe out here!"

"Nice to know we have friends in high places," came the reply. "I appreciate y'all!"

As Ken drove back to the EOC, Rob made a call to Kathy Sheetz, in DC. He remembered nothing on the list of Freschette's properties about Charleston but wanted to confirm. She informed him he was correct—nothing in their records about known-properties owned, but the Freschette holding included a hotel chain with a presence there. That's excellent news, Rob thought. He'll be back soon.

Chapter 25—Bad Moon Rising

The next few days were exciting, to say the least. Of all the craziness Rob had experienced, preparing for and experiencing a major hurricane had not made the list. I guess I can check that one off, he thought. As it turned out, Miss Rita stayed west of the city, though she brought tropical storm force winds to New Orleans and caused even more flooding. The short staff at the EOC worked their tails off. All-in-all, NOLA dodged a bullet. By Sunday, the 25th of September, most of the staff had returned and things were getting back to their usual pace—as chaotic as ever.

"Want to go check up on our buddy in the Garden District?" Ken asked Rob, as they were grabbing coffee from the large urns at the back of the EOC, "I could use some air, anyway."

"Let's roll, Ranger!" was the immediate response, "maybe I'll get some fresh intel."

Upon arriving at 2211 Prytania, it surprised the guys to find a different team of security guards in place of the four who had previously been on duty. The new men had a distinct look and feel. These guys are genuine operators, Rob thought. Different uniforms, too, though still with the BATS logo. As Ken came to a stop, one of the new guys walked to the SUV.

"How may I help you, gentlemen?" the man had a British accent. He was polite and professional, "this is private property and a closed area."

Ken and Rob flashed their City of New Orleans EOC identification cards, "We're doing a bit of post storm recon," Ken answered, "one of your team is a fellow Arkansas boy, who also served in a unit I was once with. Just checking how he weathered the storm."

"That was Merryman. He's been reassigned. Anything else?" short, not-so-sweet, and to the point.

"Nope. We're out. Have a nice fuckin' day," Ken left no doubt of his true feelings—Rob liked that. Turning to Rob, he said, "You're in a different league with these guys. They aren't 'private security,' those guys are mercs if I ever saw one—and I've seen plenty."

"Yes, Sir," Rob agreed, "Billy Badass there was obviously the lead dog. The other four guys look to be Colombian. I find that especially interesting."

"How the hell can you tell one Latin nationality from the next?" Ken was genuinely curious. "I hate to sound racist, but they all look alike to me."

"Years of practice, my friend. My time in the DEA gave me plenty of opportunity to refine the art," Rob replied, "subtle to most, definite to some. Mexicans and Colombians are both ruthless killers—Colombians are more determined fighters. This could get exciting."

"I don't want to know your plan, but you know I'll do anything to help, short of going with you. Tonight, though, we need to go to Club 1660. Marfel sent a 'special invitation.' You in?" Ken knew the answer would be yes. "By the way, they are re-opening High Tops tomorrow night! Be nice to sit in an actual bar for a change." High Tops was the bar in the lobby of the fourth floor of the Hyatt, a short walk from the EOC.

"I'm in on both missions," Rob replied with a grin, "but I prefer the second to the first!"

When Ken and Rob got to room 1660, there was a sense of energy in the crowd's vibe. *I guess it's like the feeling you get when a bullet just misses your head*, thought Rob, *serious adrenaline rush!* NOLA had dodged a very large bullet with Hurricane Rita.

Marfel and his bunch were at their usual table, once again playing Texas Hold 'em. Dennis Clancy seemed to be winning, based on the stack of chips in front of him. He looked up at Ken and Rob.

"Hey, boys! Yo, I just learned today that 'ARMY' stands for 'Ain't Ready to be Marines Yet'—is that for real?" The other guys at the table howled with laughter. Neither Ken nor Rob cracked a smile.

Ken finally did smile. Sort of. With more like a smirk, he answered, "That's funny. Truth be told, Marines were my second choice, but they're all fine in my book. Any of them are better than being a pussy that never served at all." Ken knew that not one guy at the table had so much as been in the Boy Scouts. Now Rob was smiling too. The guys at the table weren't.

"Whoa, boys, chill!" it was Marfel, "we have a few things to discuss. No harm meant, gentlemen, you know I loves me some Rangers! Pull up a couple of chairs."

Marfel laid out his latest scheme and 'special request.' The City was planning to escalate any rebuilding efforts that would be important for Mardi Gras. Mardi Gras meant tourists, and that meant revenue. Even though it was months away, it was top priority. Marfel was already 'recommending' contractors to do the needed work. He wanted Rob to get them on top of the very next PW, along with the more-needed firetrucks, ambulances and hospital repairs. This guy is such a dick, Rob thought, but I will take his ass down soon enough.

Rob and Ken listened, nodded, had a drink, and took their leave. But not before Rob took another opportunity to fuck with Big Jimmy.

"How's that knee, big guy? Any more freak accidents? Loss of balance is a sign of brain damage, you know. I'm genuinely worried about your health." Ken wondered how Rob could keep a straight face, spewing that bullshit.

"One of these nights, me and you gonna dance," Big Jimmy spat, "and it won't be the fucking Macarena."

"Well," said Rob with a big grin and a hard stare, "we already know that your two-step sucks. Maybe you should stick to the hokey-pokey." At that, Ken let out a guffaw and steered Rob towards the door, while Jimmy sputtered and turned three shades of red.

As the men walked back to the sixth floor, Ken couldn't stop laughing. "The fucking hokey-pokey? That's what you come up with? You are a hoot, amigo!"

When he got back to his room, Rob fired off an email to the FBI SAC in Houston, filling him in on the latest scheme from Marfel and his band of idiots. He included his suspicions about David Wilson being in on the shenanigans. Wilson had approved the initial Project Worksheet with the crime cameras on it and had submitted that to FEMA for payment. This next one would no doubt get the same treatment. Jay Bowden let Rob know he felt confident in opening a case against these guys, and that the FBI greatly appreciated the assistance.

SAC Bowden also let him know the FBI had arrested twelve additional people related to the retail organized crime ring. Resulting arrests recovered almost $1 million worth of electronics, jewelry, firearms and other merchandise from a warehouse near Baton Rouge. The 'baddass' Master Sergeant had flipped like a Waffle House pancake, throwing a slew of cops and Guardsmen straight under the bus. Rob had done his duty and would next be needed only as a witness when things got to court. Rob was well-pleased at the feedback from the Feds. He could now feel better about focusing his attention on his primary mission—to have a meaningful 'chat' with Dante Freschette. Before that, though, he still needed a couple of more days to grease the chute for taking down the NOLA crooks.

The next morning, Rob went back to work in the Finance Office, as usual, to find the invoices Marfel had mentioned, smack dab on top of his inbox. What a surprise, he thought. Wilson walked by, gave him a nod, and waved for Rob to follow him to his office.

"Hey man," Wilson started, "I just want you to know that me and Fred appreciate you. Your background at Arthur Anderson speaks well of your ability to see things in 'shades of gray,' shall we say? By now, you know we do things our own way, down here. Always have. But we also take care of them that takes care of us. We gonna cover you, too, don't you worry."

"I'm glad you brought that up. I wasn't sure you were part of the Club 1660 group—never see you there—so I was going to have a chat with Marfel about it. I figure some serious juice is about to flow. I'd be open to having some of that." Rob loved this part of the sting. Adding bribery to the fraud and conspiracy charges would be icing on the cake. "I'm hoping there will be at least five zeros after whatever the first number is."

"Well, you are surely ambitious, I'll give you that!" Wilson was laughing. "That part will be out of my hands. You probably need a one-on-one with Fred. But hey, long as I have you here, I had a phone call with Mr. Dante Freschette the day before yesterday. He's a big player in the new Economic Development Council and now that he's back in NOLA, he will be more involved. I mentioned you to him about having served with one of his kin. He was surprised, because he wasn't aware that anyone in his family ever was in the Army. He asked me a few questions about you and what you're doing down here. Said he might get in touch one of these days, when the dust settles."

Rob did not like what he heard. He hadn't worked undercover in quite some time and now wished he'd used a fake name. He also had expected none of these pukes to actually KNOW Freschette. Bad call on his part. Combined with the changing of the guard at Dante's house, Rob decided he needed to do two things: move soon; and tighten up his fucking act!

"Looking forward to it! He might have missed that branch on the family tree!" Rob stood and went back to his desk.

Back at his computer, Rob called up The Weather Channel. No Recon Operator worth the title ever neglected to consult the weather before conducting a mission. The worse the weather, the better the chances of success. Except maybe another fucking hurricane or tropical storm—Rob was definitely over those experiences. What he found was not great, but not terrible. Clear skies for the next week were not perfect, but the moon phase was in his favor. The coming Friday, the 30th, would be a dark night, thanks to a waning crescent moon. Rob chuckled beneath his breath. How perfect, he thought, a crescent moon in the Crescent City! His mind immediately began playing Creedence Clearwater Revival's Bad Moon Rising. He loved CCR—it was a good omen. Or so he thought.

At the end of his shift, Rob checked back in with Ken Fisher in the EOC. The two guys grabbed a bite, then headed to the newly opened bar for a drink or two. As they ate, Rob filled Ken in on the happenings of the day, including the email exchange with the SAC and his conversation with David Wilson. He let Ken know he would make his move on Freschette on the night of the 30th—four days out—and would wrap up his stealth mission for the FBI at that time. Still, Rob didn't want Ken to let the NOLA chumps know he was off the job. He might be needed to clean up a few loose ends.

"Well, brother, it has been an honor and a pleasure working with you," Ken was sincere in his words. "I'll handle the air cover for you. I'll tell them you are dealing with some personal things back in Georgetown. How long you think you'll be?"

"That, sir, will depend on how chatty our boy Dante is once I get him alone. I can't imagine that will take very long at all. Let's get that drink!"

The High Tops Lounge was hopping when the guys walked in. A lot of overdue energy being dispersed, Rob thought. Marfel and his crew waved from a banquette in the corner. The guys waved back but kept walking to the bar. There were three bartenders working, one of which was a gorgeous brunette—Rob and Ken sat near where she was working.

"Good evening, gentlemen," her voice was a sultry as her eyes, "what can I get for you?"

Ken wasted no time. "A napkin with your phone number on it, to begin with. And three fingers of Crown Royal on the rocks."

"Don't mind my horny friend here," Rob laughed. "This old dog wouldn't know what to do with a woman such as yourself. Got any Macallan hiding back there?" Rob had scanned the back bar but saw only Glenfiddich.

The woman looked confused. "What's Macallan?"

"Yikes!" Rob exclaimed. "How long have you been tending bar? It's the best scotch made!"

The extremely attractive young woman smiled. "I'm not a bartender. But I'm all you get tonight, darlin'. I'll check with Joe over there, give me a minute."

The woman returned with a half empty bottle of 25-Year-Old Macallan. "Is this what you want?"

"It most assuredly will do! How much are you going to hurt me for a drink of that fine nectar?" Rob usually paid twenty-five to thirty bucks for an ounce of Mac 25. He expected to be charged more, considering the circumstances.

"Joe says it's five dollars for a drink. Seems legit to me." her smile was dazzling.

"Leave the bottle. And what, pray tell, is your name, dear girl?" Rob presented her with his most engaging smile.

"I'm Désirée," she spoke the name with just enough of a Cajun lilt to bring out the French in it, "and you are?"

"Tout à fait approprié, pour une femme qui devrait très certainement être désirée! je m'appelle Rob. Enchanté, Mademoiselle" Rob replied, in perfect French. French was one of six languages in which he was fluent. Based on the look in Désirée's eyes, she had no clue what he'd said.

"Sorry—in English then," Rob quickly said, "what I said was, 'very suitable, for a woman who should most certainly be desired. Pleased to meet you. My name is Rob.' As you probably know, Désirée means 'desired' in French," with that, Rob extended his hand to shake hers.

Désirée smiled and took Rob's outstretched hand, "Rob, that was the sexiest thing I've heard since before the storm. You have my undivided attention, sir," her eyes spoke more than her words—and she hadn't released his hand.

"How in the world did you wind up here, gracing us with your presence, Miss Désirée? You have definitely not been in this hotel for long—I would most assuredly have noticed." Rob didn't break the eye contact, even when she released his hand.

"Joe knows people here. They needed some extra help and I need some extra cash. I live out in Metairie," the word came out 'Metry,' to Rob's ears, "we've had it bad since the flooding. I worked for Joe over at Rick's Cabaret, on Bourbon Street. I'm a dancer—an excellent dancer. You should come see me when things get back to whatever version of normal we get back to. I do my best work in the Champagne Room," she said this with an air of confidence that let Rob know she was a REALLY excellent dancer.

"You can be sure that I shall," Rob said, "but you aren't driving back to Metaire after you get off, are you? It's dark and dangerous out there."

"Oh, no. They gave us rooms here in the hotel. No hot water, but it ain't bad. I'll be here for a while. I'm guessing you are, too?"

At this, Rob felt a twinge of excitement. "Yes, Ma'am. Since you're staying here, maybe I can buy you a drink later. What time do you get off?"

"You have a date. And as for when do I get off? Hopefully, right before you do, darlin'." With a wink and a smile, the sultry brunette twirled away to serve her other customers.

"And you call me a dog," Ken said, clinking glasses with Rob, "that was smoother than the scotch you're drinking, boy!"

The night turned out nicely. Désirée—in reality, her name was Julie—had as much pent-up energy as Rob—it had been a long dry spell for them both. The next morning was a rough one, but well worth the suffering. With luck, the two would find time for a replay—hopefully soon.

Before going to the Finance Office, Rob made a call to Deputy Director Kathy Sheetz to let her know his plans and the timeline.

"I'm planning to pay a visit to our old pal Freschette, the night of the 30th," Rob told her. "I can't be sure how this is going to go down, but I wanted to make you aware. My plan is to 'convince' him to tell me what he knows about the murders I've been fretting over for the past twenty-five years. I'm convinced he was involved. I'm also convinced that he's still in the smuggling game—leopards not changing their spots and all that. If I get anything, I'm hoping DEA will take it from there."

"I'm way ahead of you. And we agree Freschette is still in the game, but more on the money side—we suspect he's financing smugglers out of South America and Mexico—and not just drugs. Trucks traced back to one of his shell companies have been intercepted smuggling illegals across the Southern border. Human trafficking is quite lucrative. He still seems to be very well-connected, though. We still can't get traction on going after him, full bore. Every time we submit a case to the FBI, it gets squashed by the Director of National Intelligence, in the 'interest of national security.' Such bullshit." Deputy Director Sheetz was obviously frustrated.

She continued, "For your situational awareness, DEA has already deployed well over one hundred special agents and special agent/pilots to assist in New Orleans. We've sent people from the Air Wing, along with the Dallas, Houston, Atlanta, St. Louis, and Miami Field Divisions. Attorney General Gonzales decided we needed federal resources to not only help in the rescue missions—we still have several DEA employees unaccounted for—but also to help get ahead of the expected surge in violent crime in the city. He gave DEA Special Agents in New Orleans the power to arrest and to enforce any federal law under any title, as opposed to just enforcing the Controlled Substances Act. None of us in DEA are aware of this ever happening in the past," Kathy paused for a beat, "as for you, I've already submitted a Form DEA-481—a Deputization Request—on your behalf. Since I'm also the ultimate approval authority, let me be the first to welcome you back to the fold, Special Agent Anderson! You have all the privileges of any other DEA Agents on the force. You'll have plenty of local support, should you need it, but I'm not informing anyone about your activities, in advance. You need to work directly through my office unless I tell you otherwise."

"Damn, lady," Rob was shocked but ecstatic, "you are amazing! I'm just glad you didn't make me run the Fitness Course before giving me the badge! Nice to be back in the family—though I'm not sure I ever really left, in my heart."

"Based on our last evening together, sir, your 'fitness' is not in doubt," Rob could almost see the smile on her face when she said that. "Just try not to actually kill everyone you encounter. I'd like someone to prosecute."

"No promises. But I'll keep you as informed as possible, when possible. I'm looking forward to another personal meeting with you…" Rob let that last comment linger in the air, "and, thank you, sincerely." With that, he pressed 'End,' on his cell phone.

The next call was to the FBI Special Agent Jay Bowden, in Houston, "Anderson here, I need to fill you in on a very recent development." Rob then explained that he was officially back on the clock with the DEA, with newly assigned extraordinary enforcement authority. The SAC was aware of the authority recently sanctioned by US Attorney General Alberto R. Gonzales, but Rob's re-appointment to the DEA was news to him.

"Brother, you do not know how good that makes me feel," the SAC said. "My life just got much easier when it comes to actions in that part of the world! We've deployed New Haven Division SAC Michael Wolf to lead the FBI mission there in NOLA. He and ICE Assistant Director Michael Vanacore are jointly serving as Senior Federal Law Enforcement Officials. The fact that Immigration and Customs Enforcement had a joint lead role spoke volumes about the Fed's concerns related to human trafficking. That said, they are literally up to their asses in snapping gators, just trying to keep things together. I'll get with them and let them know that I'll want to keep you in my org chart, for now. No sense trying to reinvent the proverbial wheel."

"Roger that," Rob responded. "I'll check with McMenimen, but I'm pretty sure Wolf will know of me. We've worked with his Connecticut offices on a couple of retail crime cases. I do have a favor to ask, though. Now that I'm empowered, I want to be the one to present the specialized bracelets to Marfel and his mob, when the time is right."

"I don't know why I would deprive you of such a privilege," Bowden couldn't restrain a laugh, "don't forget to double-click!"

Rob then reached out to Kevin McMenimen, who confirmed that he knew SAC Wolf, quite well. He told Rob that he would discretely let the FBI SAC know they had a mutual friend in NOLA, who was working as a Special Agent for DEA. Just in case things got sticky. Kevin knew Rob well enough to suspect that things would drift in that direction.

Back in the Finance Office, Rob went directly to see David Wilson. He wanted to let him know of his impending absence and to ensure Wilson that he would return within a few days. Like the rest of the idiots in Club 1660, Wilson was too stupid to be a good crook. They had all blindly put their trust in Rob Anderson, knowing nothing about him except his cover story. Rob had laid enough bullshit on them to fertilize a corn field—soon he would harvest the fruits of his efforts. He then went to Marfel's office to deliver the same message. He left Marfel's office thinking, tik-tock, motherfucker.

Rob then went to the Hyatt, searching out Captain Albers, of 3 Panther. He found the young Ranger Captain as he was leaving the EOC in a conversation with Ken Fisher. Good, thought Rob, two birds with one stone.

"Gentlemen," Rob began, "would y'all mind joining me up on the 27th floor? I'd rather not tell you all I need to tell you, down amongst the teeming masses. Twenty minutes?"

"Make it forty-five," Albers replied. "I need to give my troops a quick sit-rep. See you boys up there."

"That works for me, too," was Ken's response. "Good with you, Ranger Rob?"

"Roger that, guys. Meanwhile, I'm heading back to my room for an equipment check and a twenty-minute power nap— It was a long night!" Rob flinched as Ken smacked him on his back, almost taking his wind.

"Yeah, dude, I'm sure it fucking was!" Fisher walked away, laughing his ass off.

Back in room 606, Rob verified that all his gear was ready to rock. He put fresh batteries in his SureFire flashlight and his Armasight N-15 NVGs. He also added black paracord and black gaffer's tape to his ruck, along with four fully loaded mags, for both his Remington-Rand 1911 and his Walther PPKs. He used the scabbard-attached whetstone from his Ka-Bar fighting knife to hone the edges of both the Ka-Bar and his Benchmade auto-deploy folding knife. Rob also verified that his wire-like jeweler's saw and his non-metallic handcuff key were secure in the seams of his BDU pants—one could never be too prepared, he thought. He still had twenty-five minutes before meeting with the guys on the 27th floor. He was in a state of semi-consciousness within one minute, and fully awake and alert, exactly twenty-minutes later.

"Well, here we are, again," Rob started, "plottin' and plannin'! I want to fill you guys in on recent developments and my proposed timeline for next steps."

Rob told the two men about his call with the Deputy Director of the Drug Enforcement Administration, his deputization and his conversations with the FBI SAC in Houston, Jay Bowden. He went into no detail about the pending actions with the City of New Orleans people, but told them about his plans to go after Dante Freschette, the coming Friday night.

"Nate, I'm hoping you'll get me back with your team for the insertion. It will be a dark night, thanks to the moon phase. Timing won't get any better for me," Rob looked to Ken, "You should plan to keep the home fires burning. I need to make this as invisible as possible to the boys in Club 1660. Their time is also coming. That will be a short way down the road. Copy all?"

A double "HOOAH!" came from the two Rangers. Captain Albers said, "I'm going to lead that patrol, personally,

Ranger. You can fade out of the formation at any point that makes sense. I'll make sure that you have the appropriate cover, as necessary. Let's close the loop on Friday afternoon, to set the logistics."

This time it was Rob who sounded off. "HOOAH!" Rob poured out the last drinks of his last bottle of 18-Year-Old Macallan. He raised his glass and offered a toast:

"To Credence Clearwater Revival—there's definitely a Bad Moon on the Rise!"

Chapter 26—Extremely High Air Cover

On his way back to his room, Rob got an email on his Blackberry from Kathy Sheetz asking him to call here ASAP. Which didn't really mean 'As Soon As Possible'—it meant right freakin' NOW. He dialed her private number.

"Special Agent Anderson, I have something for you. I think you'll find it helpful," Kathy had her official voice on, "this is, like other of your current work, under the radar. I have arranged a meeting for you tonight, in Baton Rouge. You'll be meeting with retired DEA Special Agent Ernest Jacobson. Jake was the DEA agent assigned to the Barry Seal case, back in the mid-eighties. I've known him since I was a pup agent—about as long as I've known you. He's a Louisiana boy and knows a lot about Mr. Dante Freschette. He and I had a lengthy conversation today—you need to hear what he has to say firsthand. The shit gets deep on this one, my friend. Old Dante has friends. Important friends. I'll text you his cellphone number, so that you two can arrange the meeting. You should leave now. Plan to spend the night up there. I have a trusted courier flying in there tomorrow at 0600, to create your new credentials. She will have a mobile enrollment system on the plane. She will collect your biometrics, take your photo, then print and issue your ID Card and badge." with that, the Deputy Director ended the call.

Well, shit, Rob thought, so much for another evening basking in the smile of Miss Désirée. He went back to his room, changed into a pair of jeans and a tee shirt, grabbed his already-loaded ruck, and headed for Baton Rouge. He knew of Jake Jacobson, of course, and had briefly met him during his first trip to New Orleans. They had called Rob in to review financial records, prior to issuing indictment on a large drug bust. The Seal case made Jake a legend in the DEA. Rob was eager to learn what would bring a fellow old warhorse out of the bayou. Good to have the credentials, too, in case things got sketchy, as he expected they might.

As Rob approached his F-150 inside the hotel's attached parking garage, he felt a feeling that had saved his ass on many an occasion—someone was watching him. He never questioned or doubted the tingle he felt at the base of his skull. Because it was always right. He casually deployed the pop-open ignition key on his left hand, while slipping the Benchmade into the other. Smooth, natural movements, scanning the garage with his peripheral vision. As he got to his truck—backed in, as always—a robust man stepped from behind a support pillar. Fucking Big Jimmy.

"You and me need to finish a conversation," the big man was red with anger—or maybe he's about to have a heart attack, Rob thought. "Ain't nobody out here but us, and you are gonna need help leavin'."

Rob shook his head, smiled and said, "Man, I really don't have time for this right now. Can I get a raincheck? It's really not a good time."

Jimmy gave a humorless laugh but continued to approach in a shuffling boxer's stance. "Ain't no fuckin' rainchecks, asshole. But I am about to punch your ticket for you!"

Rob was now facing Jimmy, both hands at his sides. Both hands, concealing hard, pointed items. As the big man threw a surprisingly stylish left-right combination at Rob's face, the newly appointed DEA Special Agent slipped the first punch, then parried the second attack—a hard right cross—with a slap of his left hand, stepped forward at a forty-five degree angle with his left foot, and drove the handle of the unopened Benchmade AFO II auto-deploy folding knife into Big Jimmy's abdomen, about two inches above his family jewels. Six ounces of anodized aluminum, with a glass-breaker tip, driven by 180 pounds of well-trained energy. Jimmy went face-first onto the concrete floor, with what could only be described as a cross between a whimper and a squeal. The puddle that immediately formed beneath him told Rob that the bladder strike had worked quite well. The stench that followed told him that other bodily functions had also been involuntarily actuated.

Rob leaned down and softly said, "I told you, man, I don't have time for this right now. We can finish this conversation when I get back if you want. For now, though, can I call someone for you? I think you may need help leaving." All Rob got in return was a sort of whimper. Sad, really, he thought as he drove out of the garage. Nothing more embarrassing than pissing yourself in public. Except if you've also defecated on yourself. That's just plain bad.

Rob dialed Ken's number, on his cellphone, "Hey man, I think you'd best send a medic to the parking garage—fourth floor, row five. Looks like Big Jimmy had a trip and fall. He may need an ambulance, but not a coroner. They may want hazmat gear—smells like he shat himself. It's dangerous in this town!"

"CLEANUP IN AISLE FIVE!" Ken was laughing. "That fat bastard is just too clumsy! I've got it from here—thanks for the heads up. Where are you?"

"Got a call from the Boss. She's sending me on an overnight to Baton Rouge. See you tomorrow."

The drive to Baton Rouge took almost twice as long as usual, because of the number of civilian, law enforcement and military vehicles. The southbound side was even worse. Rob did not look forward to the ride back. He called the number sent by Deputy Director Sheetz. Jake suggested meeting at an IHOP on Harding Boulevard at around 2000 hours. Rob arrived and found Jake Jacobsen, waiting for him. They had agreed on this location, because it was very close to the airport and there was a Hilton Garden Inn right up the road, where Rob could spend the night.

"Rob Anderson," retired DEA Special Agent Jake Jacobsen said, "I'd like to say time has treated you well, but why start out with a bald-faced lie?" Jake extended his right hand, along with a welcoming smile, "let's get some chow and a cuppa joe—I've got some tales to spin!"

Jacobsen was most definitely not in great shape. He was missing his left leg, below the knee, wore a prosthetic and carried a cane. "It's my honor to spend some time with you, Sir. I wish we'd had more opportunity to work together, back when we were both full of piss and vinegar. I won't stroke you with all that 'legend in his own time' bullshit—even though it's true. You look like you've had a bad run, amigo."

"Fucking diabetes. I always was partial to a good steak and a Coke. And about every other thing my doctors told me to give up. By the way, have you had the steak tips and mashed spuds at IHOP? I never pass it up!" The aging agent was determined to be the master of his own destiny.

"Kathy Sheetz says you've got some intel for me," Rob was eager to get down to business, "if you've got G2 on Dante Freschette, I need it, PDQ."

"Ah yes, the amazing Ms. Kathy Sheetz. Snow White. Now, the ever-lovin' Deputy Director of the DEA. I always knew that girl had her shit wired tight. I know you were involved in her training, up at the Facility. I worked with her on a few jobs before I hung up my spurs. Kinda like the daughter I never had. We've stayed in touch, regularly. She called me up, told me about your new role—although I may have said something about you being a fucking idiot for accepting it—asked me to fill you in on Freschette, Barry Seal and some other, much darker shit." Jake turned serious with that last phrase, "What I'm gonna share with you falls smack into the 'you can't make this shit up' category."

There's a lot of that going around, lately, Rob thought.

The waitress came to take their orders. True to his word, Jake ordered the steak tips, smothered in gravy, mashed potatoes, drowning in butter, three biscuits, creamed corn and a CocaCola. Rob ordered grilled tilapia, broccoli, rice and unsweetened—'unsweet' the waitress called it—iced tea.

"Damn, boy," Jake said, "you keep eating like that. You'll die with all your limbs attached! I figure I've got one more leg to work on." With that, he let out a belly laugh. "This ain't no practice round now, is it? So, how much do you think you know about ole Dante? I know you've done your homework—Kathy gave me a run down on how thorough you are. But buddy, I guarantee you—you don't know the half of it."

Jake told Rob about the family history, which he already knew, and about Dante's excursions into South America to set up a series of businesses—which Rob did not know.

"Freschette was the money behind the dude they called 'Jungle Mike.' We busted him about when you retired in 1988. He was the front man in Colombia. Fucking guy built a vast business selling exotic animals to zoos and monkeys to researchers. He transformed a shithole outpost in the South American jungle into a thriving town with a hospital, hotel, and a bona fide airport. Hell, man, he was even in National fucking Geographic!" Jake couldn't keep from sounding a bit like a fan. "All done with Freschette Lumber money. They built a huge lumber mill down there, with over 1,000 workers, where they harvested and milled exotic woods—then hollowed out the four by twelves and filled them with Cali Cartel cocaine. We probably wouldn't have caught on to Jungle Mike if it hadn't been for an 'anonymous letter' sent from someone in Cali. My guess is, it was someone from Medellin, if you get my drift. Those two cartels were in a serious war, about that time."

Jake paused his story when the waitress showed up with their drinks. "What about Freschette?" Rob asked. "I find no record of him getting popped. Or even his involvement in any of that."

"Oh, it's in there," Jake was glaring now, "you just can't see it because of all the redactions those fuckers from Langley made. I personally submitted two Form 6's on the prick. Conveniently squashed, I might add. This guy is—or at least was—CIA to the bone. I know damn well that he was also instrumental in the Cali Cartel winning the cocaine turf wars, here in the USA. Escobar and his Medellin pukes never had a chance. But, in the spirit of never pissing in your own cornflakes, Dante kept the love affair with Escobar going through his 'Cajun Airforce' and flyboy accomplice, Barry Seal."

The waitress returned with their food, which gave Rob a chance to ponder all that Jake had laid on him. Based on his own experiences during Operation Swordfish and what he knew about not only the whole Menolos shit-show, plus all that had come to light about the Iran-Contra scams and the CIA—he did not doubt that Jake was on target with all this. But how deep was Freschette's involvement? It didn't take Jake long to dive right into that deep well.

"So, Barry. FYI—they murdered him about two miles from where we're sitting. Those Colombian boys emptied a full thirty-round clip into his car, but they only put six rounds into Barry. Considering that the fat bastard weighed around 300 pounds, these guys were definitely not well-trained assassins. Spray and pray, right? Nevertheless, it did the job. As you probably know, Escobar and Ochoa hired the Colombian *sicarios*. They were from the Medellin Cartel. Somebody ratted Barry out about his DEA and CIA involvement and that's all there was to say about that. We at DEA were damn sure that message came through our boy Dante fucking Freschette. Which is even more interesting, because the private airstrip in Ascension Parish that Barry was using until late 1980 was on

Freschette Lumber property. When he moved to Mena, Arkansas, he bought a house that was sold to him by one of Freschette's holding companies.

"There was a lot of shit flying around by the time Seal was rolling over for DEA. He personally told me about the CIA plot to screw over the Medellin boys in favor of the Cali crew. He told me about dropping guns from the CIA to the Contras—and he told me that Dante Freschette was up to his ass in it. It was Dante's idea to move Barry to Arkansas, because Dante was connected with 'the Guv' up there and that could get Barry plenty of high air cover. Extremely high air cover. The Freschette family have influenced the direction of Louisiana's ten electoral votes since the early 1900s. With Dante, it was about influencing the CIA—it's a straightforward path to follow, beginning with Reagan and Ollie North, to the first Bush presidency, to two Clinton terms, to the younger Bush. All with strong ties to the CIA. All covering Dante Freschette's Cajun ass, because the only other choice would be to do to him what we are sure they've done to hundreds of others—including Barry Seal. As I said, Rob, *extremely high air cover.* You might be on a path to 'bring him to justice,' but the likelihood of getting that fucking guy convicted—or even indicted—is slim to none. And you, my fellow ancient warrior, had better keep your head on a swivel."

Listening to the story, Rob had almost finished his meal. Jake hadn't taken a single bite. The more he had spoken, the more visibly shaken he'd become. He's scared shitless, Rob thought. Maybe I should be, too. But that was not Rob Anderson's style. Not at all.

"Jake, I appreciate all the insight. I guess if you're gonna wrestle with snakes and gators, Louisiana is the place to do it, right? I don't know how this is going to go—or even if it will go—but I'm most assuredly going to have a face-to-face chat with Dante Freschette. If I survive it, I'll buy you another meal to replace the one you aren't eating. If I don't… well… come pour a glass of 25-Year-Old Macallan on my headstone." Rob stood and offered his hand to the former Special Agent, "it's been a pleasure, Sir!"

"Pleasure's all mine, Rob," answered Jake Jacobsen. "By the way, there's a country artist out of Texas playing at your hotel tonight. His name is Buck Mallard, and he's pretty damn good—check him out, if you decide to have a nightcap." The two men went their separate ways.

Rob checked into his hotel, then went to the bar. He wasn't really interested in watching a band perform, but he needed a drink after his conversation with Jake Jacobsen. He couldn't help wondering whether this trip was really necessary, as the old saying went. Even if he confronted Dante and even if Dante confessed to wasting Cody and Gary—was he just pissing up the proverbial rope? Would it be like Jake said, 'slim to none' chance of it going anywhere? Rob decided; fuck it—I'm going after this Teflon asshole. He listened to the Buck Mallard Band play a couple of tunes, finished his drink, and bagged it for the night.

By the time Rob got to the airport for the pre-arranged 1000 hours arrival of the DEA G-IV jet, he had already touched bases with Kevin, Ken and Special Agent Jay Bowden in Houston. All systems were 'go' for Friday night. He watched the not-so-small jet land and taxi to the Signature FBO terminal, where he was waiting in the lounge. When the plane's door opened, Rob was very surprised to see none other than Deputy Director Kathy Sheetz, looking as great as ever. She came down the airstair, followed by two men, whom he assumed to be her Security Detail, and a blonde woman, whom he assumed to be the agent responsible for the credentialing process.

"Well, this is a very pleasant surprise," Rob said, with a welcoming handshake and a smile, "to what do I owe this high honor?"

Kathy took his outstretched hand. "Nice to see you, Rob. After what Jacobsen told me on our call, I felt it would be good to meet with you in person. Let's get inside to get you official. I've reserved the secure conference room here at Signature for that. Then, you and I can go back on the plane to chat about your upcoming mission."

It only took a few minutes for the enrollment agent to take Rob's digital fingerprints, a photo, have him sign a digital pad, and print his laminated ID card. Kathy made it official by swearing him in. As they were finishing, one of Kathy's security detail agents knocked on the door and announced, "He's here, Ma'am." She nodded. The door opened, and a man entered, wearing the uniform of the Louisiana State Police, a Colonel's insignia on his epaulettes.

"Rob, meet Colonel Lawrence Thibodeaux, Superintendent of the Louisiana State Police. Larry and I have worked together on many cases in this part of the world. I've told him you are working on a special project for us, but not any details about the mission. I've asked him to extend us the courtesy of deputizing you, so that you have State law enforcement authorization, to accompany your federal authorizations. He's graciously agreed to do so."

"My honor, Special Agent Anderson," the Colonel said, in a deep voice with a strong Louisiana accent, "not much we won't do for Miss Kathy, here," He produced a small Bible from his brief case, "Please place your left hand on my Bible, and raise your right hand," Rob did so, "do you swear to uphold the laws of the State of Louisiana, as best you understand them?" a wink and a smile accompanied that question.

"I do," Rob replied, stifling a laugh.

"Then welcome to the swamp, Special Agent!" Thibodeaux presented Rob with a wallet, containing a gold shield and a card with 'Special Agent Robert Anderson,' printed on it, followed by 'Direct Any Inquiries to the Office of Col. Lawrence Thibodeaux, Superintendent of the Louisiana State Police.'

After the swearing in procedures, Rob and Kathy were escorted back to her waiting plane by her security detail. The two Agents waited outside the cabin of the Gulfstream IV.

"So, Rambo," she began, "after all you learned from Jake, are you still in the hunt?"

"I wonder if I should be," Rob answered, "but I am. But I need to know—am I tugging on Superman's cape, or spitting into the wind?" Rob always loved that song. "Other than my own satisfaction—and maybe the opportunity to bust his face—will it do any good? He's still got protection from on high, according to Jake."

"I can promise you this, Rob, I will not allow any DEA 6's being buried. If you get something solid, you've got your own high air cover. 'Solid' being the operating word. I have as many friends in the media as I do in the halls of Congress. If I need to, I'll 'leak' the juicy parts to the press and let the chips fall where they may. But if you get dead, we will disavow you and the mission. If he gets dead, we don't want to know or hear anything about it, officially. I didn't tell you that. If you get in a bind, I will send in the cavalry to save your ass, though. You're family again. And I kinda like you, which also matters." Kathy leaned in, lightly kissed Rob, then said, "now-de-ass my aircraft, Special Agent Anderson. I've got shit to do."

Chapter 27—Dante

"I thank you very much for the assistance, Mr. David." Dante Freschette closed his call with David Wilson, Chief Financial Officer for the City of New Orleans. Dante had called Wilson on the ruse of checking on some pending budget and contract items but was actually angling to get more information about the fellow named Anderson that Wilson had mentioned to him. Dante didn't like people asking about him or his family, and there had been too much of that lately. He had gotten a heads-up from one of his Washington 'friends' that at least two federal agencies had been poking around for background on his past activities. David Wilson had agreed to send Dante a screen shot of Rob Anderson's City of New Orleans ID card, which included his photo. Dante would forward that to a few of his DC insiders and his private security operatives, to do a bit of digging on his own. A man in his position can never be too diligent, he thought.

He had already learned that one Robert E. Anderson was a retired DEA Special Agent, out of the Administration since 1988. Dante's sources could not get hands on Anderson's entire personnel file, so he knew nothing about which cases had been involved. Still, the digging through files in DC was ongoing.

Dante knew that Anderson's last duties were as an Instructor of Forensic Accounting at the DEA Training Facility, and that he had continued his career after retirement with a retail consulting firm called RetailEye, Inc. A fucking accountant, thought Dante, why is he asking about me? The one troubling aspect of Rob Anderson, at least in Dante's mind, was his prior life as a US Army Ranger in Vietnam. That would have given the man some unique skills—but had he maintained them for these past thirty-five years? As an accounting teacher in the DEA? Dante knew several Nam vets—he himself had avoided the draft, thanks to his family connections—but none of them were in any kind of good physical condition. Not like himself. Dante was fit and proud of it. His personal trainer kept him strong, and his regular boxing workouts gave him a sense of confidence in his ability to take care of himself. Not to mention that he was an excellent shot—and he was never without his Glock 17 9mm pistol. He also had his small army of 'Private Security' operators. Mercenaries, really. Dante had no worries about a retired and aging Ranger / Accountant. He just wished he could shake that gut feeling about the possibility of being wrong. He called the number for Garrett Edwards, his Head of Security. Edwards was a retired British SAS Sergeant Major, with vast combat experience.

"I need you to meet me in my office in thirty minutes," Dante began, "we may have a situation upon us, and I'd rather be prepared, should it materialize."

"Roger that, Boss. Just me, or the other supervisors, as well?"

"Just you, for now," Dante replied. "If you think it's important enough, you can brief your team and establish a plan of action. See you in thirty."

When Garrett arrived, Dante poured himself a drink and laid out all the details that he knew pertaining to Rob Anderson. He did not offer a drink to his Security Chief—Dante did not allow drinking on the job. He gave Edwards a copy of the photo he'd received from David Wilson, which Edwards studied intently.

"Yes, sir, that's definitely the same bloke stopped by here. I didn't give them much time, but from what I could tell, he looked fit enough." Garrett Edwards made a habit of giving everyone he met an appraisal, "looked to be late fifties or early sixties. Hard eyes, though. I reckon he's seen his share of shit."

"My contact at the City told me that Anderson has arranged for a few days off, supposedly to take care of some 'personal business' back home. Too conveniently coincidental, for my taste," Dante had long ago stopped believing in 'coincidences,' "I'd like to hear your thoughts."

Garrett Edwards looked up from the photo. "You know how I feel about anything that sounds just a bit too perfect, sir. I'll plan to add another guard to the detail and to make sure all are locked and loaded. If he comes around, it will be his last mission."

"Oh, no," Dante said, in his slow New Orleans aristocratic drawl, "I don't want him dead… well… not yet… and certainly not in this house. I want to ask him about his interest in yours truly. I'm counting on your 'special skills' to assist me in obtaining those details."

Garrett Edwards loved the 'wet work' part of his job. And, as satisfying as he found the killing, he took even greater pleasure in extracting information from unwilling people. It was an art, and he was fucking Van Gogh. He chuckled to himself, thinking of Van Gogh's cut-off ear—rather à propos, he thought. "You know you can count on me, Mr. Freschette. Assuming the man is foolish enough to show up here."

"Yes," Dante drawled, "assuming. Which I would do, Mr. Edwards, which I would definitely do."

Dante finished his Crown Royal, then went to his room. He removed his Glock 17 from its holster, checked that the mag was full and that there was a round in the chamber. He placed the semi-automatic pistol on his bedstand, did his nightly routine of showering and brushing his teeth, then climbed into his luxurious bed.

Garrett Edwards called his men together to brief them on the situation, ensuring that each had not only several mags of live ammunition for their weapons, but that each also had their tazers. He let them know that lethal force was to be the last option—but it was still an option.

Edwards then personally walked the interior of the large house, checking the security systems. Each window had a standard magnetic sensor, in order to silently alert if the window was opened. The specialist installers embedded these into the window frames, to be virtually invisible to the unaware eye. He also checked the discretely placed motion detectors in each room and hallway. All were in proper working order. *Fucking Tower of London, this is*, he thought.

The Security Chief then walked the entire outside perimeter of the house at 2211 Prytania Street. He had not chosen to deploy the garish light towers that had become ubiquitous in NOLA.

He had motion-sensing flood lights on every side of the house, powered by the generator which served the entire house. They were all working as designed, but he had a plan percolating his mind. He ordered one of his supervisors to disable every other light on the south side of the house. He wanted a bit of a lure should The Lone Ranger come around for a visit. Garrett wanted the intruder inside the house. He wanted the patches of darkness to seem inviting, but not staged. If this guy thought enough of his own skills to actually make a move on Dante Freschette in his own fucking house, Garrett figured the man's ego would overcome his caution.

Chapter 28—In the Still of the Night

It was almost 1800 hours by the time Rob got back to NOLA—traffic was insane. He parked in his usual spot, chuckling as he walked by the still-visible stain on the concrete, from Jimmy's 'induced lack of bodily function control.' When he got back to his room, he texted Captain Nate Albers and Ken Fisher, asking them to meet him in their 27th floor hideaway.

"Gentlemen," Rob began, "all systems are green to go."

Rob then took a moment to fill the guys in on some of what he'd learned, but not all of it. He shared the parts about being fully credentialed and about being deputized by Louisiana State Police—those were important, because it provided both guys cover, should things go south—they were assisting a sanctioned law enforcement agent. He did not share the information about Dante's political connections or suspicions of involvement in human trafficking. That fell, in Rob's mind, into the 'need to know' category—they didn't need to know.

"I've been giving some thought to the insertion operation," Ranger Captain Albers leaned in. "I'm thinking that we will do a three-vehicle mounted patrol. Three hardback Humvees, with me in the lead and you in the back of the rear vehicle. We will deploy from here at 2300 hours tomorrow night. I'll stop abreast of the 2211 Prytania Street house and start a conversation to hold the guards' attention. I will have my driver touch his brakes for every guard we get eyes on. You can bail out of the rear hatch of the drag Humvee and get busy. Roger that?"

"Roger all that," Rob replied, "and be sure to give your guys a big thanks from me. See you tomorrow night at 2245 hours."

Captain Albers excused himself. The two older Rangers went down the elevator to the EOC, where Ken introduced Rob to a new face.

"Rob, meet Himadri Banarjee. Himadri has just installed a new system which gives us a real-time situational awareness view of certain assets involved in the response effort. We've installed satellite trackers on some of the cop cars, ambulances and firetrucks—their locations show up on this monitor here. The device isn't in all of them, yet—this is just a beta test—but we've concentrated those we have, in the Central Business District, Garden District and Lower Ninth Ward. Himadri and I are working hand-in-hand with the dispatch desk here in the EOC, so that we can move them where we want them, like chess pieces," with that, Ken gave Rob a slight wink, "It will be a great tool, when it's fully deployed."

Rob shook Himadri's hand, then took Ken aside to ask him what all that was about.

Ken was smiling his sly smile. "Rob, old buddy, you can now be assured that no NOLA police, fire or ambulance will inadvertently spoil your upcoming party. We will have them all 'strategically engaged' elsewhere. More importantly, the trackers we are using are small and battery-powered," Ken handed Rob a small black device, slightly larger than the Zippo lighter Rob had carried, until he gave up tobacco, "can you get away with stowing this in your kit, so that we have friendly eyes on your sorry ass? As long as you are outside, the bird will find this thing—even inside, in most wood-frame buildings. It even has an 'SOS' feature—push the button under that little flap and the device will ping with a distress code."

"What is this, some Quantico magic?" Rob asked, in awe, "It's small enough that I'm sure I can incorporate it into my ruck gear. I have a couple of discrete slots for stashing important stuff. Much appreciated, amigo. Let's hope I never have to hit that button!"

"This, believe it or not, is what they call COTS—Commercial Off the Shelf—technology. Anyone can buy it. The magic is in the software used to track it. Himadri has created quite the system, with RamSafe—he's a freakin' wonder kid," Ken was obviously proud of his team—and rightly so.

"I'm happy to have this," Rob replied, "and even more happy to have you and your folks on my side. How's about we drift on down to High Tops—I need to see a particularly enchanting bartender."

The men walked into the lounge, but to Rob's dismay, Désirée was not working. The bartender told them that Rick's had reopened, along with several other Bourbon Street bars—the lovely Désirée had gone back to doing what she did best. After a drink at the bar, the guys got a bite to eat. On the way out of the lounge, they encountered Marfel and his entourage, coming in.

"Well, well," Marfel began, "if it ain't my two favorite Army Rangers!" Looking at Rob, he said, "I heard you were out of town for a bit, yet here you stand. What's up with that?"

"I have an early flight tomorrow," Rob replied, "hard to get flights when things are so backed up. But hey, I'm glad we ran into you boys. I'm going to come see you next week. I want to get some clarity on the work we've been helping you with." In his mind, Rob finished with 'and slap your scurvy asses in handcuffs!'

Dennis Clancy leaned into Rob's personal space and said, "We know what happened to Big Jimmy, asshole. He's going to be laid up for quite a while. He says you blind-sided him. I want you to know that I'm not happy about that. We will have a more pointed discussion about it, when you return from wherever you're off to."

"Hmm—blind-sided, eh?" Rob laughed out loud. "Obviously, Jimmy must be a bit embarrassed by how things actually came down. Can't blame him, I guess. The guy just can't fight. I didn't even get a good sweat on—which is fine, because I was short on time. I could use a good workout, though, so if you'd like to walk with me out to the parking garage, I'd be happy to add some of your bodily fluids to the stain where your pal lost his bladder and his bowels. I have about fifteen minutes before a call I need to make. That will leave me with ten to spare, after I finish with you."

Clancy leaned back away from Rob, and said, "Fortunately for you, old man, the Mayor is waiting for us right over there," he nodded at a table full of people, "but I'd love a raincheck. We'll see how that Ranger shit holds up to my Brazilian Jiujitsu."

"Well," Rob said with a smile, "while it is true that I have underwear older than you, I'll see if I can muster the stamina to continue this chat next week. I hear BJJ is badass stuff—thanks for sharing that with me. But you know, there was an old riverboat gambler who once offered some sage advice: 'never show your hole card'—you should remember that. See you soon, bitch."

Rob and Ken stood their ground until the pack of future-defendants moved away. Once safe to do so, they turned and walked out the door.

"I want to be a fly on the wall when that action comes down," Ken laughed, "that will be a sight to see!"

"Hell, brother," Rob returned the laugh, "I hope you're guarding my back. These asshats are not going to play by the rules. We'll figure that out when the time comes."

After dinner, Rob returned to his room. He did one last check of his gear, adding the new tracking device to his kit. The ruck had a built-in hydration bladder, and Rob fitted the tracking device alongside the outlet for the drinking tube. Good enough, Rob thought. It feels like part of the unit. While Rob had no plans for anyone else handling his gear, plans were constant sources of surprise and disappointment. Experience led him to always assume that the defecation would sooner or later hit the proverbial rotary oscillator. He filled the bladder—hydration was critical to success, and this would be hot and stressful work—and included a few energy bars, just in case. Out of habit, he once again checked his pistols and ammo and took a few more passes of the whetstone over his edged weapons. He put new batteries in his NVGs. Finally, he slid his two newly issued Federal and State law enforcement officer credentials into a discrete slit in the lining of his custom-made West Coast Shoe tactical boots. The gold shields would be too bulky to be stealthily carried. He was ready. Tomorrow, he would spend the day in his room thinking through his plans, drop his remaining gear in room 605, run through some Taekwondo forms—they always helped him to mentally prepare for combat—then lie low until time to deploy. For now, though, a solid night of glorious sleep was in order.

Friday, September 30th went as Rob hoped—quiet and uneventful. Ken stopped by room 606 with chow at lunch and dinner, also providing sitreps on the recovery efforts in NOLA, particularly in the Garden District. At 2245 hours, Rob discretely made his way to the first floor of the parking garage, to rendezvous with Captain Albers and his team from 3 Panther. Each of the men gave the figure in black respectful nods, as Albers escorted him to the rear Humvee.

"Give 'em hell, Ranger!" Captain Albers gave Rob a firm handshake. Then they were rolling.

As per the plan, Rob was watching from the rear vehicle as Captain Albers's point unit came up to the target house. He could see three guards, but the brake lights flashed five times. Then things went weird. Rob could hear Captain Albers's voice over the radio.

"Sir, get that fucking flashlight out of my face! Do it now!"

A voice with a Spanish accent replied, "Fuck you—I have a job to do—you're on my turf here!"

Nate spoke into the radio, as Rob could see him open his door, "Prepare to engage!"

At that command, four soldiers in each Humvee rapidly dismounted, with M4 rifles pointed at the guards around 2211 Prytania, who were all pointing their weapons back at the soldiers. No time like the present, Rob thought, sliding out the back hatch of the Humvee. Maybe Nate will kill all these motherfuckers and save me some work!

With the spotlights from the three Humvees illuminating the security guards and twelve soldiers wielding eleven M4 assault rifles and one M249 squad automatic weapon, it was clear that those mercenaries didn't stand a chance. Frankly, Rob hoped they were smart enough to know that, because the resulting mess would be a nightmare for the boys from 3 Panther—and it would blow his plans to hell. Most importantly, Rob did not want to be caught between them if the shit came down. As he waited alongside the Humvee, Rob could hear a Brittish-accented voice yelling:

"Stand down, stand down!" It was the guard that had rudely sent Ken and himself away when they stopped by the house. Clearly, the boss.

As the guards lowered their weapons, Rob could see that Captain Albers and the Brit were working things out. He took that opportunity to move into the garden of the house next door to his target. It was, as he expected, a dark night, especially once away from the beams of the Humvee spotlights. Rob lowered his NVG, to get the lay of the surrounding landscape. He navigated around a couple of large oak limbs which had come down during one of the two hurricanes, making his way up to a hedge-covered low fence at the rear of the two adjoining properties. From there, he watched as the 3 Panther patrol mounted up and continued their mission. He could hear the booming voice of the Brit, giving hell to his underlings in excellent Spanish, another of Rob's fluent languages. Those *pendejos* are having a rough night, he thought. I may just have to add to their misery.

Rob removed the NVG and placed them in his ruck. The 2211 Prytania house had no visible exterior cameras. There were security lights Rob had previously noted, though about half of them were out. Still, there was enough light to see what he needed to see—there was a first-floor window, near the back, which was a possible entry point. Rob thought that would be too obvious. There was a back door and a side door. There was an attached structure in the back of the building, adjoined to the main building by a covered walkway. House-slave quarters, Rob thought, from the Antebellum Period. That's my path.

He climbed over the low fence and made his way to the covered walkway, where he decided to wait for more of the house lights to be turned off. Parked next to the rear building was Dante's Range Rover. See you shortly, Mr. Freschette, Rob thought, don't wait up for me. Rob settled in, hearing the old Five Satins song, playing in his head…'In the still of the night…'

Chapter 29—The Problem with Plans

From his vantage point in the bougainvillea growing along the walkway between the former slave quarters and the main house, Rob had a decent view down the illuminated center hallway of the home. He could see from the back door to the front foyer and could see light streaming into the hallway from two of the rooms on the south side of the house. Also, he could see that a second-floor light was on, in the corner room on the north side. Rob thought that was likely to be coming from Dante's room. Regardless, he saw no guard posted directly at the rear door or inside the front door.

After about another half-hour, tucked up against the fragrant bushes, he saw the upstairs light go dark. As Rob was about to move towards the back door, he caught a shadow on the hedges directly across the large courtyard from him—a roving perimeter patrol. This did not surprise Rob—in fact, he'd expected more of them. He heard the guard's radio:

"*Unidad Uno, informe!*" came the voice on the other end of the radio.

Unit One's report was brief and to the point, "*Todo bien. Continuar patrullando.*"

That's right, Rob thought, all is good. You keep moving and all will stay good—for the moment. But it didn't stay good for very long at all.

The guard continued his slow walk around the perimeter of the rectangular-shaped courtyard. The problem was, Rob was hiding on the return leg of the path. Rob was not positioned to see the corner behind him—all he could do would be to crouch low and hope to blend into the dense foliage of the bougainvillea. He slowly and quietly drew his fixed blade knife from the sheath strapped to his lower right leg, hoping he wouldn't need it. Knives are so damn messy, he thought. When the guard was a few feet behind him, Rob heard the footsteps stop. Fuck, Rob thought. As quickly as his thought, came his action. Rob spun while still crouched low, then sprang at the shocked guard like a panther out of the darkness. Before the guard could unsling his M4 rifle or key the shoulder mike on his radio, Rob struck him with a rising blow directly beneath his chin with the butt of the hefty Ka-Bar. The guard's mouth had been opened in half surprise / half fear. The blow from beneath his chin slammed his jaw closed and his head back, with all the weight of Rob's body, driven upwards by the lunge from his crouching position.

"*Buenos noches, amigo,*" Rob said softly, as he grabbed the falling man by the straps on his tactical vest to keep him from dropping with a crash. The sound of the man's teeth slamming together had sounded like a fucking pistol shot—that was already too much noise for Rob's taste. Unless he knew a good dentist, Rob could see that this guy wouldn't have that problem again—his teeth were all but gone, from the force of the blow. Rob pulled the man to the edge of the building and placed him on his stomach, to keep him from choking on his own blood and teeth. He stuffed the man's ball cap into his bleeding mouth. Rob retrieved the duct tape from his ruck, wrapping it around the fallen guard's chin, then over the top of his shaved head, so that the man couldn't open his mouth should he regain consciousness. He used the guard's own flex cuffs to secure his hands and feet, then moved to the back door. He knew he wouldn't have much time before the team leader sent someone to find his missing soldier.

Looking through the backdoor window, Rob could see no movement down the hallway. There was light streaming in from only one doorway now, towards the front of the house. Still, his internal warning signals were all illuminated. Too easy, he thought, that's never good. He assumed that the doors and windows would have sensors to alert if opened. If they monitored the control station, it would have to be local. Few, if any, central stations were back in business—not that Dante would use such a service anyway, Rob thought, not a guy who basically had a small army at his disposal. Assuming all that, he figured he would have maybe ten seconds to get to the lit doorway. Because it was the only lighted room, he thought that was most likely the Ops Center for the guard detail. As luck would have it, that room was also at the bottom of the stairway to the second floor—and Dante.

Rob reached into his BDU pocket and pulled out two small, flat tools he was rarely without—one with a jagged edge and one with a ninety-degree angle—a lock rake and a tension wrench. He was an expert at picking locks. When most teen-aged boys focused on Boy Scout merit badges and model airplanes, Rob was teaching himself how to pick locks and throw knives. He made quick work of the old-school Schlage deadlock but waited a beat before opening the door. He walked himself through the steps: open, then close the door quickly and quietly; draw the 1911; move tactically but quickly towards the lighted doorway—stay against the wall—old wood floors are creaky; politely convince the guard to ignore the intrusion alert; prepare for the shit to hit the fan.

He opened and quickly closed the door. The shit hit the fan. None of the other steps mattered. As Rob turned to move up the hallway, he was immediately hit by a tazer, fired from a darkened doorway to his immediate right.

When Rob regained consciousness, he was taped to a rolling office chair. His first thought was: and that is the problem with plans.

# # #

Inside the EOC, Himadri Banarjee made an urgent call to Ken Fisher, reporting that the ping from Rob Anderson's satellite tracker had gone dark.

"When did you lose him?" Ken asked.

"The device automatically pings every thirty seconds. I had him in the rear courtyard of 2211 Prytania Street, under one minute ago," Himadri explained, "my guess is, he's inside. Many of those old houses have metal roof caps, embossed copper ceilings—some even used chicken wire as lathe in the plaster walls. Basically, a Faraday cage. He's probably not going to show up again until he leaves that house."

"Copy that." Ken hung up the call, then rang Nate Albers, to bring him up to speed.

Chapter 30—Twenty Questions

"Welcome back, Sleeping Beauty," Rob recognized the Brit. "I'll bet that was a shock… get it… shock? Man, I crack myself up!" The Brit stood about four feet away, laughing.

"Go fuck yourself," Rob replied, "your time is coming."

This brought even more laughter from the Brit, which then brought laughs from the two other BATS guards in the room. Definitely Colombian, Rob thought. Rob could also see a fourth man, standing just behind the very bright quartz work lights that were shining in his face. Dante Freschette.

The Brit continued, "We do have you at a bit of a disadvantage, now, don't we? I'll give you points for having balls, though. I'm still deciding whether I'll let you keep them. Frankly, I've always had respect for you Ranger blokes. Served in The Regiment, myself. Brothers-in-Arms, and all that. Won't save your sad ass, but I might feel a bit conflicted about what I do to you. For a minute or two." More laughter.

"Now, hold on, Sergeant Major Edwards," Dante's drawl was smooth as silk, "let's not get ahead of ourselves. Why, Mr. Anderson here," Dante bent down to look in Rob's eyes, "oh, yes, we know who you are, sir," he continued, "Mr. Anderson here might just save us all a mess of trouble. Rob—may I call you Rob?—I am so very curious as to why you have been asking people about me? And making up tall tales about serving with one of my kinfolks? Oh, yes—and why the *fuck*," Dante put strong emphasis on that last word, "are people in Washington, DC scrounging around in my personal records? Would you please enlighten me, Rob?"

"Well, suh," Rob spoke in his own significantly more redneck-than-aristocrat Alabama accent, "as soon as we trade places, with you sittin' heah wrapped in duct tape, I may tell you all those things," Rob only called up the accent when he felt it was appropriate, "meanwhile, y'all can kiss my Alabama ass!"

Rob's statement brought a chuckle from Dante—and a backfist to the right side of his head, from the Brit called Edwards, that almost knocked Rob's chair over.

Dante continued, "As we are in my parlor, let's play a parlor game. I'm sure you're familiar with the old game called 'Twenty Questions'—one of my personal favorites. Allow me to refresh the rules for you. It's a guessing game in which one player thinks of an object and informs his opponents whether it is 'animal, vegetable or mineral' or, in some games, such as the one we shall play, 'abstract.' Then players, in turn, ask questions designed to limit the field of inquiry and close in upon the answer. Of course, in our game, only I shall be asking the questions. Only 20 questions are allowed, usually, each phrased so that it may be answered 'yes' or 'no.' Again, our game will be a bit different. I will, in most cases, ask for some elaboration, should I choose to do so. It is my game, after all. The 'winner'—I use the term loosely—is the person who provides the correct answer; if there is no correct answer—or no answer at all… well… we will get to that part later."

"What's the winning prize?" Rob asked, never breaking eye contact with Dante.

"Ha!" Freschette backed a laugh, "that's the interesting thing. The 'winning prize' as you call it, is, you don't get viciously hurt by my associate Garrett, here. Until the next question, that is. Shall we begin?"

Rob looked at the Brit—he now knew that he was Sergeant Major Garrett Edwards, at some point a member of the British SAS—then he shifted his gaze back to Dante. In both men, he saw a similar glimmer in their eyes. They had played this game before and liked it. Rob was pretty sure he decidedly would not.

"I have a reputation for being both belligerent and uncooperative, Mr. Freschette, which, combined with my advanced years and waning memory, does not bode well for a successful outcome of this game. How would you feel about a different slant: I'll tell you why I'm here; you'll tell me what I want to know; Prince Albert here can go have crumpets and tea, or whatever. Once we do all that, I will decide whether to immediately kick all of your asses, or whether to have a drink first, then kick all of your asses."

This brought a round of genuine laughter—first from Dante, then Garrett Edwards, then joined by the two Colombian guards.

"Mr. Edwards," Dante finally said, "would you like to respond to Mr. Anderson's interesting proposal?"

The Brit stepped forward, planting a front kick square into Rob's chest. Taped to the chair, Rob rolled backwards, which he was glad of, since it lessened the force of the powerful kick. Wheels catching on the edge of the oriental rug, the chair flipped backwards. As Rob crashed to the floor, the two Colombians were on him, each with a kick of their own. They then set Rob and the chair back upright.

"Let's negotiate, Rob," Freschette was leaning into Rob's face, "frankly, I do like part of your proposed rule change. The part about you telling me why you're here. We can just call that 'Question One.' I do have others, however, which I hope you will be equally forthcoming about. But please, continue—I am intrigued!"

Rob knew he was in a bind. He needed to buy himself all the time that he could—what better way than playing out a long story. A twenty-five-year-old story. If he could drag it out long enough, maybe Ken Fisher's magic tracker would let the cavalry know that he hadn't moved in a long while. Rob hoped that while not sending the SOS, he was still sending a message: he was stuck, somewhere. He began his tale.

"In 1979, you were at a very nice waterfront home in Bolinas, California. I know this because I have photos of you there. While you were there, a couple of wannabe gangsters from the Midwest came to do a drug deal with either you or the Colombian who owned the place. My best guess is it was with the Colombian. What I also know is—from someone who was there—you were very upset about these two cowboys, because they were playing *tourista*, taking pictures of the ocean. And, as it turns out, of the people at the house, including you.

"Thing is, a couple of months later, both those guys wound up dead. Now, based on what I know of you and some of your 'past adventures,' we both understand that getting killed is not an unusual outcome in the world of drug dealing. But this one has just stuck in my craw, all these many years. Frankly, I had written those two off as nothing more than victims of a local rivalry—until the pictures showed up, just last year."

Dante interrupted, "So, let's review. You come down here, start messing in my affairs, raising some powerful eyebrows in DC—over two dead punks from twenty-five years ago? Are you shitting me?" Dante was losing his aristocratic cool, "You have no earthly idea who you are fucking with, boy!"

"I think I do, Dante—may I call you Dante?—but I'm sure that you can't wait to make sure that I really do, right?" As Rob finished his sarcastic retort, Edwards again struck him. Obviously experienced, he perfectly delivered this blow to the triple warmer seventeen pressure point, located at the joint of his jaw. The lights went out for Rob, but not for long.

Recovering from the edge of unconsciousness, Rob asked, "Shall I continue?"

"By all means, please do," Dante was again composed, "I can't wait to get to the good part!"

"I think—well, actually, I'm convinced—that you had those guys killed, because they let your buddy in Bolinas know they had kept one of the disposable cameras. I'm also convinced that the Colombian, Roldofo Sanchez Flores, probably bragged to them about you and your connections, leaving them with more information than they should have had. My theory is, those two thought they could play the leverage card—more drugs, better prices, more status, whatever. They were more out of their league than they could possibly imagine. Still, they had pictures of you spending quality time with a Menolos team member and a member of the Cali Cartel, in the same house. That not only sealed the deal for Cody James and Gary Harker—those were the two boys from Illinois, by the way—but also for Flores. By the way, nice work there—classic Colombian slice and dice. Sent just the right message to the right people, no? I imagine the Menolos boys got the idea—silence is golden!

"I'm just ball parking here," Rob continued, "but my theory is, you had your Cali pals send a *sicario* to recover the pictures and deal with the two renegades. The guys must have had a second set of the pictures, though, which your hitman got from them.

Otherwise, I figure he would have gone to their homes, ravaged the places and killed everyone he found. Am I close? Interestingly, there was apparently a third set of pictures, which came out of the woodwork twenty-five years later. And now, here I am, trying to set the record straight."

"And what was your involvement with these supposed drug dealers, who were supposedly killed?" Dante wasn't very good at hiding his concern.

"I was DEA, at the time. Not the time to tell them I'm DEA now, too, Rob thought. I was preparing to bust those guys until you changed the course of things. Supposedly," Rob smiled at Dante. Dante slapped Rob. Hard.

"Well, that explains a lot," Dante said. "I knew you were an Accounting Instructor for the DEA—I do have my sources—but was not aware that you had also been a field operative. Although, seeing you now, that makes sense to me. You are clearly no marshmallow. I'm actually developing a bit of admiration for your skills, Rob. Too bad that admiration will be so short-lived."

"So," Rob's goal was to keep the chat going for as long as he could, "I showed you mine—how about a peek at yours? Seems like you and Harvey Milktoast over here have some plans for me that don't include allowing me to call home. Care to fill in a few blanks, before you send me to the hell I so richly deserve?"

"You do have a set, don't you, Robby boy," Dante was smirking, "What the hell, why not? It might feel cathartic, to lay it out there, after all these years. Ok, here goes. I was in Bolinas, that fine day, as you see in the pictures. Flores was, indeed, a Menolos guy. One of Menolos' main contacts from Colombia, specifically, Medellin, Colombia. Norwin Menolos was up to his ass in dealings with the Medellin Cartel, who, in turn, were in bed with a certain Government Agency based in Langley, Virginia, sometimes referred to as 'The Company.' I, too, was involved with said Agency. Thing is, this Agency was fed up with the bullshit being put forth by Pablo Escobar and his low rent idiots from Medellin. That's where I came in.

"I have been doing business with the Orejuela brothers since before they split with Escobar. These guys came from a higher social background than most other traffickers of the time, so I naturally found them to be better to work with. I negotiated an 'arrangement' with our friends from Langley—the gentlemen of Cali agreed to provide a substantial contribution to support the Contra Rebels, in return for access to the same 'blind eyes' that Escobar had benefitted from. Certain powerful people in

Washington were all for that. Part of my mission was to 'win over' some of the Medellin cocaine outlets, to work with our new friends from Cali. Menolos and his band of Nicaraguans were the biggest of the big. Flores already had routes and methods for bringing product into the States. That's why I was in Bolinas—to turn them all. Obviously, this mission was intended to stay very private. The Company was not ready to burn ALL the bridges to Medellin—there was an awful lot of money in that relationship. Your boys were playing with the wrong people, my friend, at the wrong fucking time. You are wrong about Flores' sad demise, however. That was all Pablo Escobar. When we found out that Flores was playing both sides of the street—Cali and Medellin—he needed to send a message about the value of loyalty.

"Still, I would have thought you'd be more upset over the cop we had to eliminate over that mess."

"Cop," Rob asked, "what cop are you referring to?

"I think her name was Becky, or Peggy or something like that," Dante mused, "she was a State cop, if I recall. She was our inside source for tracking those two punks. She worked for us for several more years—a bit of this and a bit of that—helped our organizations to get very well established in middle

America. Sadly, she retired. So, we also retired her. Can't have any loose ends, now, can we?"

"Peggy fucking Beck??" Rob could not believe what he was hearing. "Peggy Beck? She worked for your sorry ass? But she committed suicide in '85!"

Dante laughed out loud, "Our people are very good at making accidents and suicides look so very believable. Shoot, man, I've lost count. Nevertheless, the number will go up by one, very soon.

"Garrett, we need to take care of Mr. Anderson. But not here. Call the chopper to pick us up at Zachary Park in one hour. Destination is the Atchafalaya River house in Butte La Rose." Turning back to Rob, he said, "Rob, you look a bit tired. Mr. Edwards is going to give you something to help you sleep. Propofol. Sweet dreams, my prince!"

Rob's mind was going ninety miles an hour. He was angrier that he liked to allow himself to become. Peggy Beck, he thought. There had to be more to that story. Whatever it was, I now have a genuine reason to take this motherfucker out. I'm going to cut hi…

Edwards stuck him in the side of the neck with a needle. Rob was instantly out cold.

Chapter 31—Chateau La Rose

"Ken Fisher, how may I help you?" Ken didn't recognize the number, but knew that Area Code 202 was Washington, DC.

"Mr. Fisher, this is Deputy Director Kathy Sheetz, DEA, calling. Rob Anderson gave me your number. He told me that you are informed of his current status and activities. Am I correct in that?"

Ken almost stood at attention—old habits die hard, "Yes, Ma'am," he replied, "I'm up to speed on everything. Very glad that you've called. I was about to reach out to a mutual friend of Rob's and mine, to fill him in on the latest."

Ken filled Kathy Sheetz in on the most recent development—Rob's tracker had begun to ping again and was moving north from the Prytania house. He told her he had become concerned, because there had been no signal for almost three hours.

"I wasn't aware that he had a tracker," Kathy said. "Enlighten me, please."

"We have a beta system in place, designed to track emergency assets, during the response efforts down here. We gave one to Rob just before he deployed. It only communicates—we call it a ping—with the satellite, every thirty seconds. We had a good signal until about three hours ago. He was in the back courtyard of the house, where he believed Dante Freschette to be. Then the tracker went dark. My plan was to contact Kevin McMenimen, who is tight with the local FBI leadership. If Rob hadn't shown up within the next hour, I was going to request that we rain holy hell down on that place. As it turns out, he seems to be moving now—looks like he's in a vehicle, based on the ping map. Wait one… what the fuck?… Sorry, Ma'am, but this just got weird. He's now heading northeast, but he appears to be moving at over 125 miles per hour!"

# # #

Rob came to. but did not know where he was or how he got there. Nothing. Blank slate. He could tell that he was in-motion, though, and felt, more than heard, the powerful engine and the faint 'thup-thup-thup' of helicopter blades. Cool, I'm in a chopper, was Rob's first thought. Wait—I'm in a fucking chopper! was his second thought.

The helicopter was very quiet and the floor he was on was carpeted. Which Rob knew meant that it wasn't a Blackhawk or other such military bird. His head was clearing. He reviewed his memory banks, trying to get a sense of 'NOW.' Rob played back the evening, flashing forward to entering the backdoor of Dante's house. He remembered being taped to a chair and most of his dialogue with Freschette, including Dante saying, 'Good night.' They zapped me with something, he thought, probably Propofol, based on the speed, duration and recovery aspects of the drug. He'd studied a wide variety of such agents of incapacitation during his time at DEA. Based on his current loss of short-term memories, this was a classic example of the drug they called 'milk of amnesia.'

Rob lay still, not wanting to give away the fact that he was awake. He took an inventory of his body. He had no major aches, other than feeling like someone had kicked him in the chest. Oh, he thought, someone HAD kicked him in the chest! His hands were behind him, secured with what felt to be plastic flex cuffs. His feet were not bound. Two deployable weapons, he thought, three, counting my forehead. I'm still in the game. Across from him, he saw his black ruck, laying on the floor. He wondered where his guns and knives were. He also wondered if Himadri's magic hockey puck was doing its thing.

Rob could hear two male voices somewhere behind him. More evidence that he was in a very expensive helicopter. He'd been in more than a few such birds. Usually sitting in a seat, though, he thought. As his head became clearer, he could make out the conversation.

"Permission to speak freely, sir." the voice was that of the Brit, Garrett Edwards.

"Of course, Garrett, you needn't have even asked," Dante Freschette replied, in his Naw'lins drawl, "we've been together for almost thirty years! You may always speak freely to me!"

"Sir, do you think it was wise to say all you said back there? You exposed a lot to this guy. Too much, in my opinion. So much that I ordered the 'disappearance' of the two guards that were in the room with us. No loose ends. As you know, they assigned me to you to ensure your protection—and that of my boss, in Langley. You told this guy too much about our special relationship."

Damn, thought Rob, Edwards was a CIA operative! This could get very messy.

#   #   #

"125 miles per hour," Kathy Sheetz yelled into the phone, "what the fuck is going on?"

Ken was watching the Geographic Information System monitor. He spoke back into the phone, "Yes. We are confident that Rob is in a helicopter, heading northeast, at 125MPH. That would be a serious bird, Ma'am, based on my military experience. If we weren't talking on the phone, I would have assumed that you fed folks had done an exfiltration for Rob. Since you apparently have not done so, I think we can assume that Rob—or at least his tracking device—is in a private helicopter, most likely with Dante Freschette. Which is not good."

"Can you tell where they are going?" the Deputy Director asked.

"We can tell when they stop," Ken replied, "within plus or minus about thirty seconds, depending on the previous ping. When we have that, we can pin-point the GPS coordinates. When we get that, I strongly recommend sending whatever form of the cavalry you can muster."

"We have air assets and a team ready to respond once we have the location. We can spin them up in under one hour," Kathy said. "I'm reaching out to the team leader as soon as I hang up—which is right now." She pressed 'End,' and then hit the number one on her speed dial list.

# # #

"Garret, my friend, you nor our 'fearless leaders' have anything to be concerned about," Rob heard Dante say, "everything I said was old news—buried so deep that it can't be proven. It's not like I said anything about the new line of business. Even if this puke were to live—which he most assuredly will not—he's got nothing that can be considered viable evidence. He has no official status—just some PI on a vendetta. But, as I said, he won't have the chance to say a blessed thing to anyone. That boy will be gator bait by the crack of dawn!"

The voice with the British accent replied, "Which is good, because if you'd started spewing forth about the human trafficking business, I'd be feeding your ass to the gators, too!"

Both men laughed. Rob didn't see the humor. He still lay quietly, but he was so angry now that he had to force himself not to tense up. First, the memory of Dante saying he'd had Peggy Beck killed had come back to him. Now, to hear these fuckers discussing human trafficking business… Rob was pissed… he had to control himself… for now. The men continued their conversation.

"Sir," Edwards asked, "what's your plan here? I know you won't want to kill him inside your house. I'm suggesting the boathouse, where they clean the fish. The Colombian guys that we keep on staff there have a way with knives and chainsaws."

"Spare me the details, Garrett. I've commissioned it and hell, I've even witnessed it—but I still find those things barbaric. Necessary, but barbaric. I have no problem with your approach," Dante hesitated, "but I do want to have more conversation with him, first. Don't worry, nothing overly sensitive. Not that it will matter. I'm just curious about his Washington sources. Bring him into my office at Chateau La Rose. Give me thirty minutes, then he's all yours."

Rob's mind was already playing out his options. Should he lash out with his expert kicks the moment they try to take him from the chopper? Should he wait until he's inside Dante's office? Waiting for the office is the best choice, he thought. He did not know how many people would be at the LZ when the chopper landed but based on what he overheard about 'disappearing' the two guards that had been witness to his last interrogation, he was pretty sure that there would only be Dante and probably the Brit, at his next Q & A session. He could feel the chopper slowing down.

#   #   #

"Butte La Rose, Sir," Himadri called out to Ken Fisher, "the last few pings indicated slowing down, then standing still for about a minute, now."

"Copy that," Ken said, while pulling out his cellphone. He hit redial to the Area Code 202 number. "Ma'am, it appears that the tracker is stationary, in the area of Butte La Rose—up near Baton Rouge. I'll have my guys text the GPS coordinates to you at this number. It's about 120 miles northeast, as the crow flies—well, the helicopter. Please let me know of any way we can help—and please, keep me informed."

"Thank you, Command Sergeant Major Fisher. Yes, I've done my homework. You may have saved Rob's life. Assuming we get there in time, and that he isn't dead already, that is. I'll let you know what we learn." Deputy Director Kathy Sheetz hung up, then pressed the digit '1,' on her speed dial.

"Scramble," she said, "Coordinates to follow in two minutes."

#   #   #

The doors to the chopper opened. Three men climbed inside, dragging Rob towards the door. In the event that these guys knew anything about the effects of Propofol, Rob feigned a state of semi-consciousness. He did not resist the men, as they all but tossed him into the back of a waiting SUV. They threw his ruck in, too. Idiots, Rob thought, hard to find good help these days.

The men slammed the door to the SUV as the helicopter lifted off. It took approximately five minutes to get from the helipad to the house. In that time, Rob has retrieved the jeweler's saw from its hiding place inside the rear waistband of his BDU pants and had sawn most of the way through the plastic flex cuffs. Enough so that he could easily break them when the time was right. He also squirmed his way to a position where he could touch his ruck. He couldn't open it without fully freeing his hands, but he could feel the unmistakable outline of his old Remington-Rand 1911 inside! Idiots and fools to boot, Rob thought. That's a fatal combination. He re-stashed the thin, wire-like saw, then waited. As he'd hoped, the two guards stood him on his feet and forced him towards the door to the house. Inside what was a nicely appointed office, they sat Rob down in an antique-looking armless chair, wrapping three loops of duct tape around his chest and the back of the chair. They also taped his shins to the front legs of the chair. Dammit, Rob thought, time to adapt and overcome. He was already planning his move when one guard left the room and Dante entered.

"Mr. Anderson," Dante all but crooned, "I do hope y'all had a nice rest. I'm sure you've surmised that this will not turn out well for you. And you would be correct in that, of course. Still, I'd like to ask a couple of questions if you'd be so kind?"

"You are a piece of work, asshole," Rob hid his anger with laughter. "I gotta hand it to you for chutzpah. Fire away… so to speak. By the way, where's your gay lover, Garrett?"

"As are you, my short-term friend, as are you! As for Mr. Edwards, if I were of that persuasion, he would certainly fit the bill, but he and I are both dull, boring heterosexuals," Dante leaned over his desk, staring intently at Rob, "so then, would you tell me how you were able to get access to my well-hidden files, inside the DOJ?"

This time, Rob did laugh, "Joke's on you, motherfucker. I got access to those files through accessing internal DOJ systems. We got our hands on a lot of information, most of which was heavily redacted by your handlers over at CIA. But we have enough to hurt you now, between what we can read between the lines and what you've admitted to a Federal Officer."

"Federal Officer? I have never confessed anything to a Federal Officer! You sir, are full of shit—which the gators absolutely love!"

"Dumb ass," Rob spat, "I AM the fucking Federal Officer—and your sorry ass is under arrest!"

Dante and the remaining guard broke out in laughter at that. "You are no doubt still a bit disoriented from the drugs, Mr. Anderson! But man, I do admire your nerve!"

"Inside the lining of my right boot, you will find my DEA Credentials—they reinstated me, just for you, asshole. Look for yourself." Rob wiggled his right foot, which was taped to the chair.

Dante nodded to the guard, who knelt beside Rob's right leg. The guard pulled a knife from his pocket. That's my fucking Benchmade, Rob thought. I hate a thief. The guard used the knife to cut through the duct tape around the top of Rob's boot, then removed the boot from Rob's foot. He carried the boot back to the desk. He did not re-tape Rob's leg to the chair.

Dante probed around the top of Rob's boot, finding the small slit in the liner. As Dante and the guard examined the ID cards, Rob made his move. He broke through the flex cuffs, grabbed the bottom of the chair and launched himself into a forward roll, chair and all, straight at the half-turned standing guard. As the antique chair shattered against the legs of the guard and the front of the desk, the tape around Rob's shoulders ripped loose. Rob had thrown himself forward with such force that the desk slid backwards, pinning Dante in his chair, against the wall behind him.

The guard was down, but not out. He was trying to regain his feet, but one leg was sticking out at a ninety-degree angle. He was reaching for his gun when Rob kicked out with a lunging kick with his left leg. Rob's leg was still duct taped to the leg of the broken chair. He drove the end of the chair leg into the guard's right eye socket. Rob withdrew his leg. The duct tape had ripped apart. The chair leg stayed where he'd jammed it. Rob rolled to his right, landing next to his ruck. Arms free now, he drove his right hand into the bag, grabbed his 1911 and continued his roll. Rising to a shooter's stance, he aimed the gun at Dante Freschette's face.

Dante had been trying to push the heavy desk away from his body, but his arms were pinned between the polished mahogany and the leather executive chair he sat in. With the weight of both the desk and the now-lifeless 200-pound body of the Colombian guard, he had no chance of getting free. But he was screaming.

"Edwards! Edwards! Guards! Somebody get in here!" Dante never took his eyes off Rob, and the cavernous barrel of the .45 pistol that was pointed at his face.

"Shut your fucking mouth, or I will pop you without a smidgeon of remorse," Rob snarled. "In fact, I would love to do it."

Freschette stopped yelling. He had lost all color in his face. He was afraid—very afraid. Rob felt good about that. Nothing but a week-ass punk, Rob thought.

"Looks like no one is coming, amigo," Rob sneered at the helpless criminal. "Where are they all, right now? If you shoot me a line of bullshit, I promise I will hurt you. SPEAK!"

"WAIT!" Dante screamed, with near panic in his voice, "they are all down at the boathouse, getting things ready for…"

"For butchering me?" Rob asked, as he leaned in closer to Dante's face, "I'm guessing that you were going to call them when you were ready?" Rob picked up Dante's cell phone from the floor next to the desk. "What's the number?"

"Speed dial 2," Dante replied, still focused on Rob's pistol, "what are you going to do to me?"

"What I'm going to do to you is yet to be determined—depends on how things go after you call that asshat Edwards. What I'm capable of doing, on the other hand, is what you should be concerned with. Trust me, none of it is pleasant—and I'm very good at what I do."

In truth, Rob HAD decided the fate of Dante Freschette—he just wasn't ready to share the details. He pressed the second speed dial option, holding the phone to Dante's face. The look in Rob's eyes made it clear that Dante needed to play the game. He did so.

"Mr. Edwards, come get this piece of shit. I'm through with him," Dante said calmly and convincingly.

"On the way," came the reply, "be up there in less than five."

Rob pocketed the phone, went back to his ruck, and dumped it on the floor. He needed to take inventory. He found his Ka-Bar, Walther and his extra magazines for both guns. All destined to join me at the bottom of some bayou, he thought. Missing were his very expensive night vision goggles. Some puke was having an early Christmas. Rob opened the hydration bladder compartment where the tracking device was stashed. He was hoping that Ken and his guys already had a location marked, but did not want to take chances. He activated the SOS button. Send all you've got, buddy, he thought.

Chapter 32—Case Closed?

Himadri Banarjee trotted across the EOC to Ken Fisher's desk. "We just got the SOS ping, Ken! We now know that he is alive, and that he is exactly where our last tracker ping indicated!"

"Out-fucking-standing!" Ken was instantly on his feet, "the Quick Response Force from DEA should be ready to launch. It's been about one hour since I spoke to the Deputy Director. I'll call her back, now."

"Sheetz," came the voice on the other end. "What do you have, Ken?"

Fisher filler her in on the SOS ping and confirmed the location. Kathy told him that the QRF had been airborne for thirty minutes. They calculated just under an hour of flight time. In all, that would mean that Rob would be on his own for another half-hour. Nearly two hours from the time they had determined his arrival in Butte La Rose.

"We checked the list of known properties owned by Freschette and/or his companies," the Deputy Director stated, "his family has a fish camp—actually more like a fish mansion—on the Atchafalaya River, just outside of Butte La Rose. They call it Chateau La Rose. The coordinates match up."

"Rob is no slacker, Ma'am. If he's lasted for over an hour and is in a position to actuate that SOS button, he's on his game. My guess is, there are a few people around him that are most definitely NOT on their game. Please keep us in the loop?"

"Roger that, Ken. Signing off, for now," and she was gone.

#   #   #

Rob moved back to the desk, behind which Dante was still pinned against his chair. He had the role of duct tape from his ruck in his left hand and his 1911 pistol in the other. He bent down and retrieved his Benchmade knife from where the guard had dropped it, when he fell. Rob's plan was to pull back the desk, so that he could tape Dante to his office chair, as he himself had been taped, not that long ago. Only better, Rob thought. Rob put the tape on the desk and slid his pistol back into the Kramer Leather paddle holster he'd retrieved from the ruck. He looked around Dante's desk, found his DEA ID card, and placed it in his BDU pocket. He then bent down, grabbed the dead guard by his ankles, and pulled him away from the desk. The table leg stuck up from the dead man's face, like a broken mast on a shipwrecked schooner. Crude, but effective, Rob thought, you don't see that every day.

Standing up, Rob looked into Dante's eyes. "You are in luck, amigo. I'm feeling magnanimous. As I said before, you are officially and undeniably under arrest. I have help on the way, dispatched by someone who isn't afraid of your connections. Meanwhile, I'm going to pull this desk away from you and you're going to be a nice boy and allow me to tape you to that chair you're in," Rob drew his pistol, laying it on the desk, next to his right hand. "If you decide to play not-so-nice, I will blow your head clean off your shoulders. Your call."

"You have no idea of the magnitude of the shit-storm you are about to unleash, Sir," Dante had regained a bit of his composure. He was smirking. "Whoever your contacts are in Washington, I can assure you that they are no match for my own. The things I know—and have done—have been kept well-buried, along with more than a few people who thought they could do what you're planning to do. I promise you, my overly confident friend, I will not spend a single night in any jail!

"Don't fear," Dante had a mocking tone to his voice, "now that you've quote / unquote 'arrested' me, I intend to offer no further resistance. We shall let justice take her blind-ass course!"

Rob grabbed one end of the desk and pulled it away from Dante and his chair. He grabbed his pistol and moved to the other end of the desk to fully free the trapped man. As he took hold of the desk, a door opposite him burst open. It was Garrett Edwards, holding a Heckler & Koch HK 93 semi-auto rifle with a collapsible stock.

Edwards took no time in assessing the situation, pointed the gun at Rob and fired a three-shot burst. Rob was equally fast in assessing the danger. He had grabbed his Remington-Rand 1911 and dropped to his knees behind the heavy desk. Rob heard the three .223 bullets splintering the heavy mahogany desk. He heard Edwards shouting.

"Dante—out—now! This way!"

Rob lifted his pistol above the edge of the desk and emptied the magazine, starting at where he'd last seen Dante Freschette and sweeping towards the doorway where Garrett Edwards had entered. Edwards returned the fire with three more shots—then, nothing. He heard Dante shouting in the next room.

"The fucking guy is DEA! He says there are more agents on the way. We need to get to the fast boat and get out of here—NOW!"

Rob eased around the side of the desk, reloading as he moved. As he passed the dead guard, he took the Baretta M92 pistol and three magazines from the fallen man's duty rig. Can't be over dressed at a party like this, Rob thought. He cautiously entered the large Great Room. It was filled with every imaginable hunting trophy, from wildebeest hides to an entire stuffed water buffalo. A ten-foot alligator hide was hanging on one wall and a dozen fish of various species were mounted on the others. But no human beings were in the room. Rob crossed the space, carefully peering around the frame of the open door. He could see a golf cart flying down a well-worn dirt path, with four men inside. There was another cart parked next to the house—Rob jumped in it and followed the other men as they fled. Golf cart chase, Rob thought, it's like a fucking Benny Hill skit, but with guns. Rob chuckled to himself, pleased that his warped sense of humor was still firmly intact.

Rob figured the time to be around four-thirty or thereabouts—it was still very dark, thanks to the waning crescent moon. It would get light in another hour, with sunrise at around 0700. Looking ahead, Rob saw the brake lights of the cart he was chasing, about fifty yards ahead of him. He then realized that his own cart had headlights on! Thinking quickly, Rob pulled his Ka-Bar from his belt—he hadn't had time to reattach the leg sheath—then jammed the knife into the accelerator pedal and wedged the handle against the bottom of the dashboard. He rolled out of the cart, as it sped on autopilot towards the stopped cart ahead.

All hell broke loose.

The cart Rob had been in was shredded by automatic rifle fire from at least five guns. Rob was counting muzzle flashes. Rob didn't want to reveal his position by firing back, so used the commotion to advance to the right flank the shooters, to his own left side. In the headlights of the cart he'd abandoned, he could see that the cart carrying Dante, Edwards and their cannon fodder had stopped next to a building the size of a three-car garage. Must be the boathouse, Rob thought. The former Ranger drew up next to a large machine of some sort, which gave him suitable cover within easy range of his 1911. Rob could shoot one-inch groups at fifty meters, but why take chances? He opened fire, thinking, where's the damn cavalry when you need them? It had been thirty minutes since he'd sent the SOS. Then he heard the unmistakable sound of a Boeing MH-6M Little Bird helicopter.

\# \# \#

"Deputy Director Sheetz, this is Special Agent Ron Martin, Team Leader of the QRF," the call was being patched through via satellite phone, "we are above the target and can see a gun fight in progress. Looks like it's pretty one-sided. Permission to engage?"

"Granted!" Deputy Director Sheetz shouted into the phone, "get your asses down there, now!"

The light chopper positioned itself behind the larger group of fighters, lowered to approximately thirty feet above the ground, allowing the six-man QRF to slide to the ground using fast ropes. One team member remained in the chopper, for overwatch. Two of the shooters from the golf cart turned their attention to the new arrivals, firing at the descending agents. Rob took one of them out with a well-placed shot to the head, easily visible in the still-burning headlamps of his former chariot. A shot from inside the Little Bird took the other out. Two of the remaining bad guys broke off and ran for the building they were next to. The other two turned their attention to Rob's muzzle flash, sending bursts of automatic rifle fire to where they'd seen the fire from Rob's pistol. But Rob was no longer there.

The QRF Team was wearing NVGs—they were quickly able to identify Rob, recognizing that he was the one-against-everybody-else guy. They turned their focus—and their firepower—on the remaining two guards. Rob heard one painful scream and then shouts of *'No Mas, no mas!'* from one of the men. Rob was running for the boathouse. He kicked through the door and saw two men silhouetted by the dashboard and running lights of a large boat, with three very big motors on the stern. One of the men fired up the monster craft, filling the room with a deafening roar. That's Edwards, he thought, too big for Freschette. Just at that moment, the other man opened up in Rob's direction with another submachine gun. Rob dropped, rolled to his right, settling into a prone position and put three rounds into the shooter. The bigger man turned, but it was too late. Rob had pulled the Beretta from his waistband, emptying a full magazine into the big Brit.

Rob ran to the boat. His shot placement on the Brit left no facial features identifiable, but it was definitely Garrett Edwards, late of the Central Intelligence Agency. He turned the other man over… it was not Dante Freschette.

"DEA!" came the shout, as the QRF Team made entry to the boathouse, "Drop your weapon and get on your face!" Rob had six red dots squarely on his chest.

"I'm Special Agent Rob Anderson," he shouted, "I'm DEA! Stand down!"

One agent hustled over to Rob. "ID, now!" the Agent barked, shining his headlamp in Rob's face.

Rob was glad that he had retrieved his ID from the top of Dante's desk. "Right front pocket of my BDUs! Come on, man, the main attraction has done a David Copperfield on us!"

One of the Agents found a switch and turned on the lights inside the boathouse. The men split into two-man teams and began a meticulous search, inside and out of the boathouse and inside the compartments and hold of the watercraft. No Dante Freschette. That's when Rob noticed the SCUBA gear. A cubby set up to hold four tanks and four wetsuits—except there were only three complete sets in the space.

"FUUUCCKK!!!" Rob screamed at the top of his lungs, "Get that bird cruising the surface of the river—Dante is in the water!"

Special Agent Ron Martin, the QRF Team Leader, spoke via his throat mic to the chopper pilot, directing him to drop low and do a slow, careful scan of the river, both north and south of the Chateau La Rose compound. He then placed a call on his satphone and handed the device to Rob.

"Anderson," Rob barked into the phone, "Sheetz, I presume?"

"Yes, it's Kathy. Are you alright? Any extra holes we need to worry about?"

"I'm good—it's a bit of a mess down here, though, and that bastard Freschette has disappeared. I'd like to have more agents to help us with a search." Rob's frustration was obvious.

"Sorry, Rob," came the reply, "this operation was 'off the books,' so to speak. Stealth mode. I can't redirect more agents without stirring up an enormous mess. I will make a call to our friends in the Louisiana State Police, though, to see what they can do. The thing is, Freschette owns a lot of local politicians—I'm not sure how trustworthy they will be."

Rob filled Kathy in on the overheard conversations about human trafficking. She directed him to go through the house to see if he could uncover any supporting evidence. She also anointed him as Team Leader for the agents he had currently assigned to him, so that there would be no need for further check-ins from Agent Martin.

"I'll take what I can get," Rob responded. "Martin seems like a solid operator and his team are solid troops. Oh, FYI, one of the dead guys is definitely a covert operative out of CIA.

They will, no doubt, disavow that, but it still might get sticky for you. Not to mention that if Freschette HAS gotten out all this, he will be calling in his chits—you need to watch your ass."

Rob handed the satphone back to Martin, filling him in on the new command structure. Agent Martin nodded his agreement, then had one of the other agents give Rob his throat mic and radio. The sun would be up very soon, and Rob wanted Dante. Two smaller boats were docked alongside the powerful Scout 380 speedboat. Rob directed two of the QRF Team members to search Dante's office and one to guard the surviving security guard. He ordered two other team members into one of the smaller boats and took one of the agents with himself in the other boat. They left in opposite directions, searching the river and shorelines for signs of Dante Freschette.

About a mile up-river, Rob saw what he was looking for – a SCUBA tank, almost hidden in the bushes along the riverbank. Rob steered the small boat to the shore, while the agent with him covered the shoreline with his M4 rifle. Once ashore, Rob could see the footpath to what appeared to be an abandoned shed, or shack, about thirty yards inland. The DEA men approached the building, using a cover and advance tactic. Arriving at what proved to be a garage, they saw fresh tire tracks leading away from it, into the cover of the Atchafalaya River swamps.

Rob dialed Kathy Sheetz, on the satphone he'd taken from Special Agent Martin. "He's gone," he said, "Freschette has gotten away. He obviously had an exfiltration plan. I'll contact you when I'm back in New Orleans."

By the time Rob and his partner returned to Chateau La Rose, the first of the Louisiana State Police cars were arriving. Rob assigned one of the DEA Special Agents to stay behind to help process the scene and deal with the paperwork. He and the other five agents loaded up in the Little Bird, sitting on the door sill, feet on the runners. Rob instructed the pilot to go up river, cruising low and slow over the area leading away from the garage from where Dante had made his escape. The flight reminded Rob of his many chopper rides, back in Nam. He always loved the agility of the 'copters and respected the skills of the pilots. The pilot he had today was equally impressive.

Skimming just above the tops of the cypress trees, they followed the dirt road until it hit blacktop. From there, they decided that the most likely path Dante would choose would be towards Interstate 10 and the Butte La Rose Rest Area. From there, he could either head west, towards Lafayette or east, towards Baton Rouge. It didn't matter. Traffic was thick, in both directions. Rob ordered the pilot to return to New Orleans.

As much as it pained Rob to think it, this case was definitely not closed.

Chapter 32 — 1660 Takedown

On the flight back to NOLA, Rob reviewed some of the documents that the team had taken from Dante's office. Unfortunately, there was nothing which could be considered incriminating, at least not to his eyes. Maybe folks back in Quantico could make more of it. He called Kathy Sheetz, as soon as they landed, filling her in on the last twenty-four hours. Twenty-four hours that seemed both like a microsecond and a month. Combat was like that.

"I'm just glad that you're still in one piece, Rob," Kathy said, with genuine concern. "Are you ready to get back to Georgetown?"

"I have a couple of unfinished tasks, down here," Rob replied, "I need to take out some trash. Out of curiosity, are you searching the house on Prytania, too? Surely that asshole left something that can be used against him?"

"Oh, we are on it," she replied. "And we just learned that CIA has issued a 'Red Notice' on Freschette, via Interpol. That means his air cover has been officially cancelled. If they do catch up with him, my money is on 'shot while attempting to escape'— I do not expect that he will ever get the chance to say what he knows, to anyone. At least that's something good."

"I'd love to do the honors. Just let me know when and where," Rob meant every word. "Signing off, for now. I'll let you know when I'm home."

The next morning, Rob walked into the EOC, searching out Ken Fisher. He found the tall man in his usual place, drinking large cup of black coffee.

"Well, if it ain't Ranger Rob!" Ken was beaming. "You look like shit. I can only hope the other guys—there had to have been more than one—look worse."

"Rest assured, SarMajor, the survivors do look worse!" Rob winked and smiled. "But now, I have some unfinished business, right here in River City. I'm going to catch a few Zs, but I'd like your company for a visit to Club 1660, tonight. You game?"

"Oh, hell yes!" Ken exclaimed. "I'm sure things will be quite interesting!"

Rob then walked to the ballroom that was used as the HQ for the 82nd Airborne. He flagged Captain Nate Albers to the door, rose to full attention, and snapped a perfect salute.

"As you were, Ranger!" the Captain said, "no need for formality between us!"

"This one was heartfelt and well-deserved, Ranger Nate. I owe you. I don't forget my debts. I'll be out of here by this time tomorrow. I just wanted to thank you and your troops, for all your support!" The two Rangers exchanged a handshake. Rob returned to room 606, showered—he was surprised to discover that the water was hot— and immediately went dead asleep.

Rob awakened from a dreamless sleep at around 1730 hours. His body ached. He understood why. The greatest injuries an old man suffers, he thought, comes from thinking he's still a young man. Still, there was no time to wallow in it. He got up, went through a twenty-minute yoga routine, dressed, and headed out to meet Ken Fisher in the EOC. On the way, he called Special Agent in Charge Jay Bowden, in Houston.

"As you've no doubt heard by now, I'm not dead," Rob began, "but the day is young. I'm planning to drop the hammer on the gang of idiots here in NOLA, tonight. I have a team of trustworthy DEA boys to give me a hand in taking out the garbage."

"Whatever you need, Special Agent Anderson," came the reply. "let us know, if you need backup."

Rob then contacted Special Agent Ron Martin, filled him in on room 1660 at the Hyatt, and asked him to have his team in the hallway of that wing at exactly 1900 hours.

"They'll know when to breach—the signal will be unmistakable." Rob signed off.

Ken Fisher was waiting when Rob arrived at the EOC. The two brother-in-arms grabbed a bite to eat, and Rob laid out his plan.

"I've invited a few special guests to the party, tonight. They will arrive at 1900. You and I will have had the opportunity to… shall we say, 'chat'… with the pukes, prior to their entry. Which I expect to be sudden and quite rude." Rob was grinning ear to ear.

"Any chance that I might have a discrete moment of my own, with one of those boys?" Ken asked. "It would be a shame if Marfel accidentally tripped and fell… into my right fist." Both men laughed at this.

"He does strike me as a clumsy fucker," Rob replied, with a wink.

At 1815 hours, Rob and Ken entered Club 1660. They were pleased to see that Marfel, Clancy, Wilson and Jimmy were all there, but no one else.

"Boys, how's your day been going?" Ken asked, barely hiding his sarcasm.

Clancy replied, "We are doing just fine, old man. From the looks of your pal there, he probably can't say the same." The men all laughed at this.

"My walker slipped, and I fell," Rob spoke, smiling. "I'll survive it. Better yet, asshole, here's your chance to take advantage of this weak, injured old man. You did say you wanted a piece of me, right?"

Dennis Clancy stood up, pushing his chair back and out of his way. "You just lost any chance of getting cut in on our business, shit head, but you won a serious ass kicking!"

Clancy almost made it around the table, before being intercepted by Rob's spinning heel kick to the side of his head. He dropped like a bag of rocks. Shaken, but not unconscious—which disappointed Rob. I need to work on that, Rob thought.

Big Jimmy started to stand up.

"Sit the fuck down, Jimmy, or I will hurt you. I'll make you think our last little party was all cupcakes and lemonade." Rob's tone was calm and flat, but his eyes said all that needed to be said.

Big Jimmy sat down.

Marfel stood up. Ken Fisher punched him in the mouth.

Marfel sat back down. Hard.

David Wilson stood in a corner, hyperventilating.

Clancy rolled over, rose to his knees, and pulled a snub-nose .38 from his waistband.

Rob pulled his Remington-Rand 1911 and aimed it at Clancy.

Marfell pulled a Glock 9mm from beneath his jacket and pointed it at Rob.

Fisher pulled a Baretta M92 from the small of his back and aimed it at Marfel.

  Rob threw his DEA Shield on the table and shouted, "FREEZE! DEA! You are all under arrest for conspiring to defraud the Federal Government!"

Clancy and Marfel dropped their guns on the table, staring with shock and surprise at the gold badge.

Right on cue, the door burst open and four men in DEA SWAT uniforms entered, led by Special Agent Martin. All pointed suppressed M4 carbines at the men around the table, painting a ruby-red dot on each of them, center-mass.

"ON THE FLOOR, NOW!" The SWAT leader's voice was loud and forceful.

The four bad guys hit the deck, face down—just like in the movies.

Rob looked at Ken Fisher and said, "You're right, partner, these motherfuckers are too stupid to be good crooks. Let's get a drink!" Tuning to Martin he said, "Welcome to Club 1660, brother. You can take it from here."

Rob and Ken high-fived each other, laughed, and made their way to the High Tops Lounge.

Chapter 33—No Loose Ends

Four days after the bust in room 1660, Rob was back in Georgetown. Deputy Director Kathy Sheetz assigned him an office in Quantico, so that he could complete the mountain of paperwork which inevitably followed a mission as complex as the one he had just finished. Not Rob's favorite part of the job. On his way to the DEA Headquarters, Rob called his old pal, Bobby Spragg.

"Bobby, I think we can close the James Gang case. I wish I could tell you that the guy responsible was either in jail or dead, but I can't. I do think that he's on ice, though." Rob wasn't thrilled with the news he had to tell Bobby next.

"There's something else. I also learned that the death of Peggy Beck was not a suicide. She was working for the cartels, as a mole, specifically to keep tabs on the guys they were fronting large quantities of drugs. Cody and Gary were under her watchful eye, right until the end."

Bobby was crushed by that last news. He had known Peggy for decades. He thanked Rob for the closure and extended an open invitation for Rob to come for a fishing trip with him.

When Rob arrived at the DEA facility in Quantico, he went straight to the office of Deputy Director Kathy Sheetz.

"Welcome home, Special Agent Anderson," Kathy said, with a smile. "I know you're going to be quite busy for a few days, but I thought you'd like an update on our latest activities. Based on your reports and snippets of evidence found in Dante's two homes, we got a friendly judge to issue search warrants for his company offices, in New Orleans. When our agents entered the place, they found it completely trashed. The agents were specifically interested in the offices of Dante's lawyer and accountant, which were on the same floor as his own offices. All the paper files were water damaged beyond recovery. Weird thing is, not a window was broken. Also, the computers were all gone—even the server in the IT room. Local cops blamed looters. We all know that's bullshit."

"What about the lawyer and the accountant? Rob asked. "Did you round them up?"

"Neither has been seen since before Katrina hit the city," Kathy said. "They've vanished. Or, more likely, alligator bait. In my opinion, this was a classic clean up job. I think you can make a good guess at who did the cleaning."

Rob could guess. He figured it was a very experienced cleaning company, based in Langley, Virginia.

"What else?" he asked.

"We've frozen all assets of Dante Freschette and all his holding companies in the US, "she replied. "Interpol has done the same with his international accounts. If he's still alive—which I doubt. Our friends don't like unfinished business or leaving loose ends."

"Here's to no loose ends!" Rob raised his coffee cup in a toast. "And as for unfinished business, I do believe we have some of our own. Why don't we get back to that, right after I buy you dinner, tonight?"

Kathy Sheetz smiled. "And before I cook you breakfast, in the morning."

Afterword

Thank you for taking time to read my first work of fiction. Though, not all of what you've read is actually fiction. The Case is framed around the unsolved murders of two men I knew, many years ago, Gary Harker and Cody James. Their killers have never been caught, or even identified. The circumstances of their murders, as described in my book, are real. The rationale behind their murders, and the people I've described as being involved, are a combination of my own speculation and pure fiction. Maybe someday, we will know the real truth.

Most of the DEA operations described in my book were actual. I've changed most, but not all the names, however. Privacy is a right, until it's surrendered to the public. The elements of my book related to the CIA and the Iran-Contra / drug smuggling connections are based on heavily reported statements, made by a wide range of people, and supported by what was said, and/or unsaid, in the CIA Office of the Inspector General's report that I discuss in the text. The CIA, of course, has denied everything. Then again, that's their job, isn't it?

Dante Freschette is a figment of my own imagination. I came to dislike him, as I hope you also did!

The antics in the City of New Orleans are loosely based on actual happenings. You can have some fun with Google, on those things. I changed names – and elected not to name the penal institutions which were homes to some of those whose names I changed.

I used the names of many of my friends in this book, in roles that I felt they would have fun with. Some, I asked in advance. Others, I surprised. No one told me to cease and desist – yet!

Our hero, Rob Anderson, is also based on a real-life person. Me. Partly truth; partly fiction. I'll leave it to you, dear reader, to decipher which is which.